Donald MacKenzie and ͳ ..uruer Room

〉〉〉 This title is part of The Murder Room, our series dedicated to making available out-of-print or hard-to-find titles by classic crime writers.

Crime fiction has always held up a mirror to society. The Victorians were fascinated by sensational murder and the emerging science of detection; now we are obsessed with the forensic detail of violent death. And no other genre has so captivated and enthralled readers.

Vast troves of classic crime writing have for a long time been unavailable to all but the most dedicated frequenters of second-hand bookshops. The advent of digital publishing means that we are now able to bring you the backlists of a huge range of titles by classic and contemporary crime writers, some of which have been out of print for decades.

From the genteel amateur private eyes of the Golden Age and the femmes fatales of pulp fiction, to the morally ambiguous hard-boiled detectives of mid twentieth-century America and their descendants who walk our twenty-first century streets, The Murder Room has it all. 〉〉〉

The Murder Room
Where Criminal Minds Meet

themurderroom.com

Donald MacKenzie 1908–1994

Donald MacKenzie was born in Ontario, Canada, and educated in England, Canada and Switzerland. For twenty-five years MacKenzie lived by crime in many countries. 'I went to jail,' he wrote, 'if not with depressing regularity, too often for my liking.' His last sentences were five years in the United States and three years in England, running consecutively. He began writing and selling stories when in American jail. 'I try to do exactly as I like as often as possible and I don't think I'm either psychopathic, a wayward boy, a problem of our time, a charming rogue. Or ever was.'

He had a wife, Estrela, and a daughter, and they divided their time between England, Portugal, Spain and Austria.

Henry Chalice

Salute from a Dead Man
Death Is a Friend
Sleep Is for the Rich

John Raven

Zalenski's Percentage
Raven in Flight
Raven and the Kamikaze
Raven and the Ratcatcher
Raven After Dark
Raven Settles a Score
Raven and the Paperhangers

Raven's Revenge
Raven's Longest Night
Raven's Shadow
Nobody Here By That Name
A Savage State of Grace
By Any Illegal Means
The Eyes of the Goat
The Sixth Deadly Sin
Loose Cannon

Standalone novels

Nowhere to Go
The Juryman
The Scent of Danger
Dangerous Silence
Knife Edge
The Genial Stranger
Double Exposure
The Lonely Side of the River
Cool Sleeps Balaban
Dead Straight
Three Minus Two
Night Boat from Puerto Vedra
The Kyle Contract
Postscript to a Dead Letter
The Spreewald Collection
Deep, Dark and Dead
Last of the Boatriders

Three Minus Two

Donald MacKenzie

An Orion book

Copyright © The Estate of Donald MacKenzie 1968

The right of Donald MacKenzie to be identified as the author of this
work has been asserted in accordance with the Copyright, Designs and
Patents Act 1988.

This edition published by
The Orion Publishing Group Ltd
Orion House
5 Upper St Martin's Lane
London WC2H 9EA

An Hachette UK company
A CIP catalogue record for this book is available from the British Library

ISBN 978 1 4719 0579 7

www.orionbooks.co.uk

For Félix Martí-Ibañez, MD
with affection and appreciation of
his constant encouragement.

Hamish Hunter

20 February 1967

HE PUSHED through the revolving doors, flicking snowflakes from his beaver hat. He was a tall man with restless blue eyes and graying hair that needed cutting. He crossed the lobby to the Reception Desk, his sheepskin-lined coat trailing from his hand. The head porter reached into the rack behind him. He produced a key and an envelope.

"Your flight ticket, Mr. Hunter. Everything is confirmed. Thirteen hours twenty at the airport."

He smiled, pocketing the bill Hunter gave him and disappeared underneath the counter.

"From Mr. Rybak."

A card was pinned to the small bunch of carnations. *Fraternal greetings and farewell. Rybak.* Hunter nodded thanks. The interpreter supplied by the Union of Journalists had been efficient and observant.

The hotel was postwar Warsaw. A steel-concrete-and-glass unit that could equally well have been government office or factory from the exterior. The lobby was rectangular. Fake leather sofas were set down the middle, back to back. Hunter glanced across. The plainclothes Security Militiaman was still at his seat opposite the entrance, smoking a cheroot over a lowered newspaper. The man neither spoke nor appeared to listen, watching each revolution of the doors with eyes like a lizard's.

The elevators were self-operated. Hunter rode one up to the ninth floor. The corridor was carpetless, the floor covered with a rubber composition that deadened sound. Signs in Polish, French and English pointed the way to the fire escapes. He unlocked his room. The outside temperature had dropped to ten below zero. Mosaics of ice patterned the storm windows. The atmosphere inside was starved of oxygen. He turned a knob on the air-conditioning panel and threw his things on the bed.

He went through to the bathroom and put the flowers in a tooth-mug. He'd spent the afternoon in a hate-museum where, twelve hours a day, jackbooted Nazis strutted across the screen — Stukas dive-bombed defenseless villages — the camera panned through barbed-wire fences, holding on the faces of the living-dead. He scrubbed his fingers carefully and went back to the bedroom. His hairbrush lay on the dresser. His hands fell slowly as he stared. A snapshot had been tucked into the frame of the mirror. He reached for it, studying the picture with bewilderment. It showed two boys, bulky in ice-hockey uniform, grinning at one another under raised sticks. The photograph was twenty-six years old, the place a school in Switzerland. One of the boys was himself at eighteen. The other his roommate for four years, Pawel Poznanski.

He carried the picture to the bed. He sat down, remembering a towhead streaking up-ice, yelling for the puck. Two months after the picture had been taken, he'd been whipped back to Canada by an anxious mother. Time and distance completed the break-up of the friendship. He'd never heard of Pawel again. He turned the snapshot over. The edges were tattered as if it had been carried in someone's pocket for a long time. His own signature was scrawled across the top, Poznanski's underneath it.

He looked round the room as if expecting Pawel to step out of the clothes closet, his grin and machine-pistol English miraculously preserved in time. His eyes rested on the head of the bed. He noticed that his pajamas had been disarranged. He pulled them towards him. Something had been tucked in the breast pocket of the jacket. He pulled the square of paper out and unfolded it. The text was in English and typewritten.

Be on Wybrzeze Kosciuszkowski at ten o'clock tonight. Make certain you are not followed. P.P.

He was on his feet immediately, excitement replacing his bewilderment. Then it *was* Pawel — how and why didn't matter. He tore the message in pieces and flushed them down the lavatory. He glanced at his watch. A quarter to eight. He'd eat downstairs, find another way out of the hotel afterwards. He opened the street map provided by the management. Wybrzeze Kosciuszkowski was the embankment on the Warsaw side of the Vistula. A small park lay between it and the river.

He went downstairs. There were half a dozen shops at street level. The restaurant lay behind these. The bar formed part of the garishly lighted room. The hotel was popular with actors from the nearby Theater of Culture. A group of them was sitting at the bar. Bristle-haired men in high-necked sweaters wearing spade-handle beards — the women with eloquent hands and slanted eyes set in dead-

3

white faces. One of them turned her head as Hunter climbed on the stool. Her slow stare was exactly like Wanda's, he thought. Neither rude nor curious but a natural expression of interest. He ordered a scotch, making the barman pour till pale gold liquor covered both ice cubes. He drank it slowly, reminding himself that he had to buy scent at the duty-free shop in the morning. The drink finished, he went to his table. The old waiter who served him hobbled over rheumatically. He flapped his napkin at the tablecloth.

"Are steak, are *bigos*, are *kielbasa z kapusta*. All very good."

The information was standard and repeated daily. Hunter chose the last dish and ordered another scotch. He watched the old man totter away. He took the snapshot from his pocket and laid it on the table face-upwards. The waiter was back in a few minutes with a steaming dish of sauerkraut, cooking-sausage and streaky bacon. He placed it in front of Hunter, moving the snapshot without even looking at it. Hunter finished his meal leisurely, pausing on his way out to have a word with another journalist — an American with one of the agencies. The sofas in the lobby were crowded with people who used the hotel as a meetingplace. The hatchet-faced plainclothesman was still at his post. A couple more of them were supposed to be dotted round the hotel. Rumor among visiting newspapermen had it that the manager himself was a member of the Security Militia. All rooms assigned to foreigners were said to be bugged, all cables filed subjected to an unexplained delay.

He bought a newspaper at the stand and carried it up to the mezzanine floor. He sat at a table near the balcony above the lobby. He read for half an hour, sipping a cup of bad coffee. It was half past nine when he went down to the Reception Desk. He blocked a yawn ostentatiously, nodding at the hall porter.

"I'm having an early night. If there are any calls tell the operator not to put them through. Take a message. I don't want to be disturbed."

He rode up to the ninth floor. The sheets on his bed had been turned back. As far as he could see, nothing else had been disturbed except the flowers. These had been placed on his bedside table. He picked up his hat and coat and glanced out along the corridor. Empty. He hung a DO NOT DISTURB sign on the door handle and walked quickly along the corridor. His feet made no sound on the floor of the service stairs. Push-bar doors on each floor gave access to outside fire escapes. He opened the one on the second floor, pulled it shut after him and wedged it with a piece of paper. Ice made the iron staircase dangerous. He went down carefully, hanging on to the handrail. He found himself in a yard littered with all the junk of a two-hundred-room hotel. Crates, garbage cans, the bicycles and scooters of the kitchen staff. He kept out of the way of the steamed, lighted windows. The intense cold stiffened the hairs in his nostrils, putting a band of steel round his temples. He pulled the flaps of his fur hat down, covering his ears. The small door to the street was undone. He stepped out and walked rapidly south.

Overcrowded streetcars hurtled by, bells clanging, spraying slush onto the sidewalk. Small luminous boxes over the entrances identified shops and cinemas. He passed one large sign advertising the Central Department Store. There was none of the colored-neon extravaganza of Western advertising. He turned the corner, the wind off the river icy in his face. The cold made it difficult to breathe. Overhead, stars glittered in an endless black sky. He slowed his pace, scanning the faces of the passing pedestrians. They hurried by, wrapped in scarves and fur hats. None showed any sign of interest in him. Streetlamps marked the sweep of the Vistula. He stopped under a tree, lighting a cigarette clumsily with gloved hands. There was no one behind him. Five minutes past ten. He walked on with growing uneasiness, imagining leather-coated *Bezpieka* watching him from the shadows — the curt summons — "Passport!"

He swung round, hearing the noise of running feet. A boy shot past, his face barely discernible in a woolen balaclava. Hunter retraced his steps to the corner. Another five minutes had passed. He'd give it till quarter past. A woman stepped from behind a tree in front of him, taking his arm naturally. She spoke in quick English.

"Look down and smile at me, please."

She urged him on, her fingers tight on his sleeve. She was young, no more than seventeen, head hidden in her duffle coat hood. He had a glimpse of wide steady eyes, lips without makeup.

"Keep looking in front," she said, "and talk to me."

He shortened his stride, tucking her arm under his. He managed a few banalities, resisting the urge to turn round. A cab came up fast. The driver swung into the curb and stopped. It was an old-model diesel Mercedes. The meter flag was down. The driver's cap was pulled low on his head. He kept his motor running, his eyes on the mirror. The girl pulled the door and dragged Hunter in after her. The cab shot forward. Hunter's toes curled as they went into a front-wheel skid that bounced them from the edge of the sidewalk.

The driver wrenched the cab into a straight line. They drove on, past Hunter's hotel, heading for the *villégiatures* to the northeast of the city. He lit a match, holding the flame near the girl's face. She dropped the hood, showing short blond hair cut like a boy's. The illusion was uncanny. The same thin straight nose and brilliant blue eyes. Only the mouth was different. The smile on this one was stretched and anxious. The match went out. He used another for his cigarette.

"You're Pawel Poznanski's daughter?"

"Yes. I am sorry. It had to be done this way."

He nodded as if what she said was utterly reasonable. They were traveling fast along a wide new thoroughfare. The driver threaded his way through the trolleybuses, using his horn. The back of his head was young. More than that, Hunter couldn't see. The rear axle shuddered as the man changed gear. Hunter looked at the girl. She was watching him silently. He flicked ash into a receptacle.

"Are you taking me to see your father?"

He felt her move beside him. Her voice was level as if she had trained herself to say the same thing again and again till all trace of emotion had been obliterated.

"My father is dead."

The words shocked him deeply, giving him a sudden feeling of vulnerability. He hid it under a show of brusqueness.

"What's your name?"

"Celina. Please, I would like a cigarette."

He took one from the pack and lit it for her. She held it like a beginner, her fingers trembling a little. He glanced out of the window. They were already far from the city center, still driving under a festoon of trolley cables. The street lighting was sparse. He watched a couple of Security

Militiamen leave a bar, sinister in overcoats that reached to their ankles. She shook her head quickly as though realizing his doubt.

"Please trust me. We are going to a friend of my father's."

He felt for her hand and squeezed it. "Don't worry. You'll tell me when the time comes."

He leaned back, listening to the grinding half-shaft and wondering how long it would last. She opened the glass partition and said something in Polish to the driver. The cab swerved onto a secondary highway. A sign was bright in the headlamps. He saw the name SRODBOROW. There were no lights at all now — no more than silent fields backed by pinewoods. The cab turned right into a narrow rutted lane winding past trees. There was a glimpse of an iced lake beyond them. They lurched over old packed snow into a farmyard. Low buildings surrounded it on three sides. The driver turned round, taking off his cap. He was two or three years older than the girl.

"My brother," she said. The introduction was unnecessary, the likeness was unmistakable.

No lights showed outside the house. Cattle stirred as they crossed the yard, picking their way across a frozen morass. The door opened as they reached it. The man inside was holding a submachine gun with a silencer attached. He lowered the barrel, bolting the door after them. It was completely dark inside the house. The girl took Hunter's hand, guiding him along the passage. Boards creaked. He heard a dog growl. The man in front turned a door handle. Light came from two oil lamps hanging on the wall, glinting from copper cooking utensils on a massive dresser. A potbellied enameled stove burned in the center of the room. On top of it was a coffee pot. There were chairs, a table and a camp bed. A yellow-eyed dog with a spiked collar lay on the dirt floor near the stove. Its tail lashed as it recognized the man with the submachine gun. He put the weapon on the bed and bobbed his head at Hunter.

"Korwin."

He was in his forties with dark eyes set in a peaked face drained of color. His clothes looked as if they had been soaked and then slept in. He wore no tie and his shirt cuffs and collar were filthy. His boots were the reverse — spotless and made of kidskin. He took Hunter's coat and hat and hung them on the horns of a stuffed elk head. His nose twitched like a rabbit's. His English was perfect, the delivery slightly lisping.

"You know who these two children are, Mr. Hunter?"

The boy and girl were sitting close together, their faces in shadow. His hand covered hers on the table. Hunter took the chair Korwin gave him.

"I know," he said shortly.

Korwin moved the dog with a foot and sat down on the end of the bed. He unfastened a cheap suitcase and pulled out a couple of mimeographed sheets. His smile showed an expanse of stainless steel teeth.

"But you don't know who I am and this bothers you. It is natural. You must forgive our dramatic approach. It was necessary. I will tell you why." He held up the top sheet of paper. "This is in Polish. I'll translate. It is a notice circulated to the Security Militia and dated twentieth January, this year. 'WANTED FOR TREASON — Pawel Poznanski, aged nineteen, Celina Poznanski, aged seventeen.' Then it gives their description. The circular ends like this. 'Hold and secure.' "

He dropped the page on top of the blanket and picked up the second sheet. "This one is marked 'Top Secret. To all Field Security Units and Overseas Agencies. WANTED — Jerzy Korwin alias Bernard Lecky, aged forty-two.' Then they give *my* description. It goes on: 'This man is highly dangerous. His arrest must be notified immediately by telephone or radio to Warsaw Headquarters. Under no circumstances will the prisoner be allowed contact with anyone but a member of the M.B.' You notice that the wording differs in each case. The message is the same." He drew his finger slowly across his throat.

Smoke drifted from Hunter's nose. He shifted his chair a little. It was hot by the stove. The dog raised its head as Hunter moved. Korwin silenced its growl. He touched the butt of the submachine gun.

"I cannot afford to be caught, Mr. Hunter. Perhaps I would talk this time. They have new ways of persuasion. Do you know many Poles?"

Hunter tapped ash into the base of the stove. "I'm going to marry one. You say you might talk — what about?"

Korwin fished in the cardboard suitcase again. He showed Hunter the sheaf of pages ripped from magazines. Titles and layout were familiar. Each page had been torn from copies of Hunter's magazine. The articles were his own. Some of them went back five years. Korwin threw the sheaf back in the suitcase.

"Just to show why we are trusting you. You are an enemy of oppression and Pawel Poznanski's friend. I too was his friend." He came to his feet and walked behind the boy and girl. He laid his hands on the boy's shoulders. His voice was quiet.

"Tell Mr. Hunter how your father died, Pawel."

Snow shifted on the roof, dislodged by the heat of the stove. It slid down, landing with a soft thud outside. Hunter kept his eyes on the boy's face, listening to the halting English.

"My father was Engineer Pawel Poznanski. My father is being arrested fourteen November in Cracow. Is being taken M.B. headquarters. Is three days without food, sleep and water. Are taking out teeth and nails with pliers. My father is dying upside down, choking with own blood. Is not saying anything to anybody." He had the same tense restraint as his sister. Their linked hands were shaking.

Hunter moved his head, shocked by the boy's manner and the beastliness of the statement. He spoke with quick compassion, addressing Korwin.

"You want me to help — how?"

Korwin held the boy tight for a moment then returned to his seat on the bed.

"There are idealists left in Poland, Mr. Hunter — but prisoners dreaming of escape. Just dreaming. Pawel Poznanski wanted more than escape. He wanted the destruction of the system that held him prisoner. There are others like him. Men and women willing to sacrifice everything but honor. They need help. In England I can find this help but not without you."

Hunter glanced at the table involuntarily. A trick of lighting heightened the girl's resemblance to her father in a way that was uncanny. Korwin had to be a member of a professional intelligence system. The British maybe. Once arrested, he'd be left to talk his way out of it. Failing that, written off as a dead member.

He pitched his butt at the stove. "I already told you. I'll

do what I can to help, of course, but I'm a newspaperman. I'm not in the espionage trade. On top of that, I'm leaving for London tomorrow."

Korwin's smile was apologetic. "I know that. We knew of your arrival, too. We are leaving Poland as well, Mr. Hunter — the three of us. Once I'm on British territory, I am safe. But for these two children I need political asylum. What I want you to do is to present certain information to the right people."

"And who are the right people?" Hunter asked bluntly.

Korwin turned his hand from side to side. "Military Intelligence. Five years ago, I could have done better than that — given you the name of a contact. Not any more. The dead are forgotten, Mr. Hunter. But you are a newspaperman. You will find a way to do this discreetly. And above all I stress the need of discretion. More lives than just ours depend on it. Vodka, Celina!"

The girl took a bottle from the snow outside the door. She polished four small glasses and placed bottle and glasses on the bed beside Korwin. There was no hint of bluster in his face, nothing but an assurance that seemed total. As if the decisions of the Fate Sisters had already been accepted. He poured vodka into the glasses. They stood as he raised his own.

"*Zdrowie!*" He placed the bottle by Hunter's chair. "Take it with you. It will remind you of us."

Hunter sat down. "With the wagonload you have to haul, what chance do you think you could have of escape?"

Korwin's voice was confident. "With your help, the chances are excellent. There is a concert in East Berlin on Sunday — in the Palace of Cultural Achievement. *Orbis —*

the official Polish Travel Agency — is organizing two special trains to Berlin. We have tickets. The police control will be light — it is a cultural outing for comrades, remember. Rest assured that we shall not be recognized. There is a house in Potsdam where we can wait in safety. That is as far as we can go alone. Deliver our message and the rest will be done for us."

The boy and girl were side by side again, watching every move that Hunter made.

"Why didn't you go to the British Embassy?" he asked curiously.

Korwin shook his head. "The *Bezpieka* have been waiting for me to do just that for ten months. Diplomats in Warsaw are suspicious, Mr. Hunter. London would have to be consulted. By the time a decision was taken, we'd be hanging from our heels like Pawel Poznanski. No. Circumstances governed our course. Your visit to Warsaw, the concert in East Berlin. And something else. I spoke of the forgotten dead — it wasn't said bitterly — that would be foolish. But I *am* returning to life. It is necessary for me to signal my arrival."

Hunter digested the import of the words. "What's that mean?"

Korwin leaned forward on the bed. "At midnight on Sunday, a hundredweight of explosive will go off in each of the six main power stations in Warsaw. We have waited a long time. The moment is ripe. We have the right men in the right place at the right time. I shall set the charges myself. Delayed detonation will take care of the rest."

Hunter lit another cigarette. "Let's go back to the house in Potsdam. The three of you are waiting there. For some reason or another no one turns up to rescue you. What happens then — you're no better off, surely, in the Russian Zone than in Warsaw?"

Korwin ticked off the points on his fingers. "The Potsdam address is contained in the information you'll take with you. Some of our men are engineers. There's an expert assessment of the damage the sabotage will cause — an estimate of the time needed for repairs. Finally, there is everything that London needs to contact me by radio. Call signal, frequency and time. If there's any delay for any reason, I can be reached here till Saturday night. Failing a warning, the three of us will be in Potsdam. Failing a warning, I use six hundredweight of plastic explosive."

Hunter stretched his arms, the last doubt gone. In the twilight world of opposed ideologies, anything was possible.

"Count me in," he said simply. "Where's the message you want me to take?"

Korwin flashed his steel smile again. "In your hotel room. Look in the pocket of the suit in your clothes closet. We gambled heavily on you, Mr. Hunter. We had no alternative. Don't worry. The chambermaid is a friend. You'd better go now. The cab must be returned before midnight."

He helped Hunter on with his coat. The girl came over. She stood before Hunter, her eyes downcast. Suddenly she seized his hand and kissed it, curtseying. When she looked at him again, her eyes were steady but brimming.

"The picture of you and my father — it was mine. I would like you to have it."

She went from the room quickly before he could answer. Korwin took the submachine gun in his right hand and opened the door to the corridor. Outside the house it was

14

even colder. An animal moved in the nearby woods, the sound plain in the rarefied air. Korwin gave Hunter a few last instructions and went back to the house. It was twenty to twelve when the cab stopped on the corner of Hunter's street. It drove off quickly towards the university. The door at the back of the hotel was locked. Hunter walked round the block to the front. The lobby was empty. He pushed through the revolving doors. He was halfway to the elevators when he heard his name called. The hall porter's face was curious.

"Do you have your key, sir? It's not on the hook."

Hunter nodded and walked away, knowing the man was still watching him. He closed his door, leaving the key in the lock. The curtains were drawn tightly. He opened the closet and felt in the pockets of the gray suit. His fingers touched two small disks wrapped in tissue paper. He took them to the light and tore open the paper.

The rain drove diagonally between the airline bus and the plane, blurring the lights in the distant terminal buildings. He watched from the head of the steps, waiting for the caped hostess to give the signal to disembark. The ground crew scuttled about, water pouring from their yellow slickers. The hostess raised her arm. Hunter ran down the steps to the bus, shielding his head with a folded newspaper.

He took a position near the door. A bearded rabbinical student stumbled myopically up the steps after him. A couple of American girls followed, wearing coats with sleeves emblazoned with badges. They were young, blond and very sure of themselves. The thin-faced Englishman behind them shielded himself from their exuberance with his briefcase.

15

The elderly Polish woman who had sat next to Hunter smiled at him timidly. Rain drummed against the windows. The noise stopped suddenly as the bus pulled under the shelter of a concrete canopy.

They climbed the long ramp up to the main floor. A brilliantly lit corridor stretched ahead. Heavy plate glass windows lined it on both sides. Pelting rain spattered the glistening tarmac. The scream of jet engines followed the disembarking passengers along the corridor. A succession of waiting rooms showed behind the windows on Hunter's left. The people trapped there sat patiently under a bombardment from public address systems.

The group from the Warsaw plane divided into three files. Most of the passengers turned left. Immigration Officers waited to inspect holders of United Kingdom passports. The Polish woman and the rabbinical student disappeared into the Transit Lounge. The rest of the passengers lined up under a sign reading ALIENS AND COMMONWEALTH CITIZENS.

Hunter surrendered his passport to the man behind the desk. The official studied the photograph briefly and flipped over the pages. The visas seemed to interest him — the Brazilian more than those of Eastern European countries. He was a youngish man with a pale face and the eyes of a policeman. His voice pitched somewhere between congratulation and envy.

"You certainly see the world."

Hunter shrugged. "I get paid for it."

The man flicked back to the title page, reread Hunter's particulars and surrendered the passport reluctantly.

"Thank you, Mr. Hunter."

The next hall cornered the incoming passengers between

the Immigration Officials and their colleagues in the Customs Hall. Here were lavatories, closed-circuit television screens and a battery of stand-up telephones. Ground hostesses sat behind glass enclosures, aloof with superior knowledge. Habit took Hunter to the message board. He scanned the envelopes rapidly. There was nothing for him. That meant that Wanda was waiting outside, almost certainly.

A notice came up on the television screens. A metallic admonition through the speakers reinforced it.

"Passengers traveling on Polish Air Lines Flight 239 from Warsaw should now proceed through Gate 4 for customs examination."

Hunter pushed his hand into his coat pocket. Fingers found the two sixpenny pieces. Each had been drilled hollow and reconstructed. Their weight was correct to a gram. He could open the coins blindfold now. Finger and thumb held the center. A quarter-turn on the milled edge unlocked each piece. He unclenched his fingers, letting the coins fall back in his pocket.

His one bag was already up. He claimed it and walked across to the bench. Three Customs Officers were chatting together, their nautical uniforms somehow out of place in an airport. One of them strolled over to Hunter, carrying a printed card in his hand. He put it down beside the Canadian's bag.

"Is this all the luggage you have, sir?"

"Everything," said Hunter.

Shrewd eyes appraised Hunter. "Where are you resident?"

"Right here," said Hunter. "In London."

The man's finger jabbed down at the printed card. His gaze never left Hunter's face.

"Then I suppose you're familiar with this notice?"

Hunter's grin came naturally. "I know it by heart."

Bags were being lifted onto the bench on each side of him. Their owners registered either nervousness or a manner calculated to impress with their innocence. A lone figure lurked near the screen by the exit — the roving Customs Official watching for some last-minute fumbling in clothing or handbag, the briefcase posed casually where it might escape inspection.

"All I've got," declared Hunter, "is a bottle of vodka — already opened."

"No scent or cigarettes?" persisted the officer. "No gifts for friends in this country?"

"Nothing," Hunter answered steadily. He'd forgotten to buy scent. "Just the bottle of vodka." It took an effort to keep his hand out of his coat pocket.

The officer bent as if to mark the bag with the chalk in his hand and then thought better of it.

"Let's have a look at this vodka."

Hunter opened his bag. He unfolded his pajamas, revealing the bottle of spirits. The measure of four glasses was missing. The Pole's lisping voice sounded in Hunter's memory.

"It will remind you of us."

The Customs Officer dug beneath the clothing, feeling his way round the bottom of the bag. His curtain of suspicion lifted temporarily. He chalked a hieroglyphic on the end of the bag.

"OK."

Outside a group of people was waiting for people off the

Warsaw flight. A man raised his hand in greeting. He was in his mid-thirties with pale hair cut short. Eyes like washed pebbles stuck in cement gave him a slightly aggressive look. He wore a dark suit and carried a soaked umbrella. He grabbed Hunter's bag with his free hand.

"Hi, Hamish! Great to see you! How did it go?"

Hunter grinned wryly. "If I didn't know Toronto, I'd say 'fantastic.' But with Dunn, anything can happen. Is Wanda here?"

"Sure thing." Borgerund nodded at the soaked vista beyond the enormous windows. "I rode out with her. She's in the car. You know what creeps these airport police are."

They made their way past the bookstall and bank counters to the escalators. Hunter stood a step above Borgerund, looking down at the top of the other man's head. The scalp was freckled like the back of Marty's hands. There was method in the way he stood, poised and ready to step off with the right foot. Another time-and-motion study, Hunter thought sourly. Marty had been coming up with them all this last year. Bugging the bureau staff with little ploys that were designed to save useless fractions of time and energy. Somebody was going to have to tell him about it.

"I got the usual treatment," Hunter said impulsively. Whatever else, Marty meant well. "Hand-picked interviews. Complete freedom to see and hear whatever they wantd me to see and hear. Nevertheless, we just might have done it this time. Incidentally all your statistics checked out, more or less. A little more than less."

Borgerund glanced back over his shoulder. "Why wouldn't they — I earn my salary. Anyway, for once we had the wind behind us. Nothing's broken here that's likely to run us out of the feature spot. What were the women like?" His full mouth was smiling.

Hunter stared back steadily. "I didn't have time to notice."

Borgerund stepped off the escalator precisely. He touched the umbrella to his chest in mock apology.

"Excuse *me!*"

The small red car was parked beyond the bus shelters. The two men raced towards it through the rain. Twin wipers swished arcs on the wet windshield. A girl's face glimmered behind, framed in dark hair worn straight to her shoulders. Her eyes slanted beneath a low fringe. Hunter dragged open the door and let Borgerund in behind. He took his place beside the girl at the wheel. She touched his cheek with long nervous fingers.

"Mmm! You've been away from me too long, darling."

She was wearing a camel's hair coat with epaulettes, zipped boots and high-necked sweater. Hunter shoved his legs out as far as they would go. Borgerund's presence bothered him. Marty seemed to be making a threesome of it too often these days.

"Too long," he agreed. He waited for her answering smile. It came with all its old excitement. Her lips barely divided at first then widened almost savagely. The chunky amethyst ring he had given her was on her left hand. The car smelled, sharp-sweet with Ricci's *L'Air du Temps*. He had given her that, too. All the signs were right. Suddenly he felt home again — relaxed, in spite of the coins in his pocket.

She rammed into low gear, spinning the car into the traffic with assurance. Her voice was low and modulated.

"We missed you, Hamish."

He filched a cigarette from her handbag and cupped his hands round the match. The salt burn of French tobacco invaded his lungs. He spoke between coughs.

"Who 'we'? I didn't know I was that popular!"

She followed the flashing trafficator to the outside lane, overtaking expertly.

"Stop fishing for compliments. You've been away for three weeks. I want to know what you've been doing — *everything*."

It was no more than a show of her usual interest. Possessive curiousness. Yet he had a swift sensation of uneasiness. He was a bad liar even by implication. But he had to lie and go on lying till released from his promise.

"What do you want to hear about?" he parried. "Collective farming, the Central Park of Culture or the beautiful Tartar interpreter from the Union of Journalists? Mine had seven children and his name was Rybak."

She flicked a sideways glance at him. "Poland," she said quietly.

His eyes sought the road ahead. "Poland," he repeated. "I didn't see anything I'd have recognized from your father's description, if that's what you mean. No serfs knuckling their foreheads. 'Forests where I am riding dawn till night, seeing always *my* land — *my* pipple, Hemmish.'" He dropped the travesty of General-Count Yampolski's accent and added, "nothing like that."

Her body shifted. Her voice was very quiet.

"Have you been sleeping properly?"

"Sure, I've been sleeping properly," he lied. "And I've been drinking properly just in case anyone's interested."

He felt Borgerund's fingers touch his shoulder. The only sounds in the car were the whine of the small motor and the hiss of tires on wet macadam. He pounded his right fist into the palm of his left.

"All right, all right! I'm sorry."

The apology was false. His outburst had been deliberate. But it achieved its object. Nobody mentioned Poland again. Signals stopped the car at Hammersmith Broadway. A cab drew alongside, riding with its meter flag up. Marty spoke hurriedly.

"OK. I'll grab this, Hamish. Get a good night's sleep, hear now? I'll see you in the office in the morning. There's no hurry. I checked with Ginny. There's nothing on your desk that can't wait." He climbed out over Hunter and jumped into the empty cab as the signals changed.

Chelsea was sad under the continuing rain. The red Mini turned left past the Royal Hospital onto the Embankment. Bridges that were already strung with lights reached across the swollen river into the twilight. A hundred yards west, a small apartment building fronted a triangle of soaked grass. One bare plane tree stood in the middle of the patch. Wanda drove into the forecourt. There was a sign over the entrance. BLAKE HOUSE.

She cut the motor and leaned forward, her hair falling in front of her face. He pitched his butt through the window and imprisoned her wrists in his hands.

"What is it?" he asked gently. She shook her head without answering. "What's the matter, darling?" he insisted.

She freed herself, swiveled the driving mirror and adjusted the collar of her coat.

"Nothing. You're tired. I'd better go home."

22

He lifted his bag from the rear seat and opened the door. "You're going *nowhere*. I want to talk to you."

It was warmer inside the small entrance hall. The houseman had laid a strip of protective matting across the carpet. A couple of hunting prints hung on the yellow-washed walls. A plant with red flowers grew in a pot on top of a brassbound chest. Left and right of the staircase were two doors. Hunter used a key to open the one on his right. He closed it behind Wanda and pressed the light switch.

The large room was out of proportion to the rest of the apartment. A refectory table stood parallel with the end wall. The portable typewriter on it was almost hidden under books and magazines. The shelves behind the table carried more books, jammed haphazardly wherever they would fit. The two windows were draped with blue curtains. No one in the block used the patch of grass outside. In summertime, sparrows bathed in the dust at the foot of the plane tree, indifferent to the houseman's neutered Persian. Sometimes a haze hung over the river, blanketing the hooting of the passing barges. It had been a good place to work.

He riffed through three weeks' mail, discarding bills and circulars. The bank statement was more or less what he expected. More than five hundred pounds in his sterling account, six times as much in the dollar account. It was the first money he had ever saved — without too much difficulty, yet grudgingly. He turned on the wall heaters and drew the curtains. He stood for a moment, watching Wanda.

"Will you marry me, Countess Yampolska, darling?" he asked suddenly.

He went through to the kitchen without waiting for an answer. Wanda had been in while he was away. A bundle of clean laundry was on the table, fresh milk and some had-dock in the refrigerator. He ran water over the tray of ice cubes, tipped them into a bowl and returned to the sitting room. She had taken off her coat. It lay on the couch beside her. Her legs were drawn up, the tan corduroy skirt wrapped round her knees. He uncorked the bottle of vodka and cov-ered ice in two tumblers. He added a little more liquor to his own glass. Her face was expressionless as he toasted her in the phrase she had taught him.

"Twoje zdrowie, kochanie!"

She stared into her own glass, clinking the ice slowly from side to side. After a while her head lifted. Her dark hair and gold sweater accentuated the whiteness of her skin.

"What made you say that, Hamish? You don't really want to marry me."

He tipped his coat on the floor, straddled the chair and leaned his chin on the backrest.

"I love you. Good enough answer?"

She shook her head, looking at him thoughtfully. "Not entirely. You've been saying as much yourself for more than two years."

He emptied his glass and replenished it from the bottle on the floor. The vodka made a pool of warmth in his stomach. He smiled.

"But I've seen the light. I'm a man with a strong sense of family. Added to which I happen to have seventeen thousand bucks in the bank."

She touched the edge of the glass with her tongue, frown-ing.

"You know I can't marry you. At least not now. I have responsibilities."

He tapped himself on the chest. "*I'm* your responsibility."

She shook her head slowly. "You're not being fair. My father relies on me — people at the club."

He drew a cigarette from the pack with his teeth and lit it. Rain lashed the windows but the big room was cosy. A room that was as much hers as his, he thought suddenly. The sheepskin rugs were her contribution, the Impressionist prints, the icons over the fireplace. They had been lovers here, losing the world over long winter weekends, the doors locked and the phone left unanswered.

"The club!" he said in a voice grown bitter. "A hangout for broken-down cavalrymen, too aristocratic to think except in terms of the past. Conniving to get the last cent out of people who have been supporting them for twenty years. That's a *great* idea, not being able to walk out on your father. That I like especially. What do you think would happen to him — wouldn't he find any more suckers for his chemmy games?"

Color flared under her high cheekbones. "I don't have to listen to your insults. You're forgetting that. Nor do I *have* to give reasons."

He drained the last dregs and gave himself a refill. It was just after five, too early to be sure of reaching Benstead. And whatever happened, he had to be reached that night. He crossed the room, bent down and pulled the hair away from the nape of her neck. He kissed the skin, whispering. She lifted her arms in answer, imprisoning his head and holding it fiercely.

He carried the bottle and glasses across the hall. The wide bed dwarfed the white-painted room. A tartan rug was spread over it. He sat down, kicked off his shoes and padded over to the dresser. He emptied his pockets, bundled the suit into a cleaner's bag and hung it on the back of the door. He heard water running in the bathroom and tiptoed back to the dresser on impulse. He separated the two sixpenny pieces from the rest of the coins and climbed between cold sheets. Reaching for the bottle, he cut the light. He turned on his back, letting the vodka trickle through pursed lips. He put the bottle down as the bathroom door opened.

A glow from the two-bar heater bathed her naked body. She ran to the bed as he threw back the covers. He found her mouth with his, pinning her with his weight, oblivious to everything but the urgency of their bodies.

He woke from a doze, sensing movement in the dimly lighted room. A clothes closet covered the opposite wall. One of its sliding doors carried a full-length mirror. Wanda was standing in front of it, fully dressed, brushing her hair with long steady strokes. He raised his knees and drank from the bottle, using the mound of bedclothes as cover. He dropped his legs, knowing she was watching him in the mirror.

"I work hard," he said defiantly. "My system gets tight. I need to relax."

She continued to brush her hair, still watching him. "You're trying to convince yourself, not me."

"Why don't you go ahead and say it?" he challenged. " 'I can't bear to see you like this, Hamish. You're deliberately destroying yourself. You don't drink as other people do. With you it's a sickness.' "

She turned, walked across the room slowly and put his brush back on top of the dresser. He tilted the bottle again, making a face at her. The gesture defied a hundred winks, the silence in his office that greeted the announcement that he was going out for fresh air.

"Shall I tell you the *real* reason why I drink?" he asked with leaden emphasis. "It's in order to hang on to some sort of illusion about myself. To reassure myself I'm not the sort of guy people take me for."

Impatience flickered in her eyes. "What are people supposed to take you for?"

Ash dropped from his cigarette. He brushed it away, staring down at the gray streak left on the sheet.

"A typewriter for hire — a literary whore."

She shook her head slowly. "What absolute nonsense! On top of that you're being sorry for yourself. You sound ridiculous."

Her tone brought him bolt upright in the bed. "I sound ridiculous, do I? Let me tell you something — people like your father have been whining about Free Poland for the past twenty years. Suppose I told you I'm doing more for his cause than the whole bunch of you — would that sound ridiculous too?"

Her eyes widened. *"You?"*

"That's right, me." He realized that he was speaking aggressively but was unable to stop himself. "Why look so startled?"

She crossed the room slowly and sat on the end of the bed. "What are you trying to tell me?" she said in a low voice.

The bottle slid through his fingers to the floor. "No more than this, baby. Your father's a fake. Patriotism isn't just a matter of running up the flag and saluting every time someone else buys champagne. It's blood, sweat and tears. *Sacrifice*. Thank God there are still people in Poland who understand it. I've met them."

She was twisting the amethyst ring round and round on her finger.

"What are you going to do — *write* about them?"

He leaned back against the pillows. "They don't need publicity. All they need's the assurance that when they make their move for freedom it won't be wasted."

She looked up, leveling dark blue eyes on his. "Who could give them that — assurance, I mean."

He swung himself out of bed. "A good question. Don't look for an answer." It was almost seven. He had to shave, dress and collect his car.

She followed him into the bathroom, standing by the tub while he soaped his body. Her voice was still quiet but insistent.

"Why do you treat me like a child? My brother's brains were knocked out by a Pole — a Communist. In front of his own mother. Doesn't that give me the right to hate them?"

He stood up, playing the shower nozzle on his back. He faded the temperature till he gasped under the icy spray. The shock sobered him.

"It gives you a reason, not a right. Let's forget it."

She wrapped a heavy towel round his flanks and dried him. "You don't trust me. Is that it?"

He rinsed the taste of drink from his mouth. "That's it. I don't trust you."

He chose a gray flannel suit, silk shirt and black knitted tie. The image for Benstead had to be the right one, one of sober respectability. Anything less would defeat his purpose. He

28

tied his shoes and gave them a wipe with a rag. He took money and driving license from the dresser. She was in the front room. He uncapped the pinch-bottle and dropped in the two sixpenny pieces. They lay indistinguishable from a hundred others. He donned his mac and put the lights out.

Strains of Verdi came from the apartment opposite. Mr. Plummer conducted his hi-fi set every evening, seven through eight, complete with baton. The gesture was his personal defense against celibacy and the rigors of Board-of-Trade routine.

They ducked through the rain to the red Mini. Wanda switched on the motor and sat staring through the windshield. A brewery sign blinked on and off in the wet darkness across the river. Her voice sounded tired.

"Where do you want me to drop you?"

"The garage." Already he imagined someone waiting in the shadow for them to leave. A drenched figure that would slip silently into the apartment and make straight for the dresser. Hunter groped for a cigarette. Finding none, he invaded her handbag again. The sooner the proper people took over, the better. Twenty-four more hours of this would have him peering under beds like a scared slavey.

"Are we seeing one another tomorrow?" he asked suddenly.

She turned into Flood Street and drove towards the lights of King's Road.

"That depends whether or not you want to. I'm free at five."

He inhaled deeply. She was playing the misunderstood woman. The thought that he was supposed to feel a heel angered him. His voice was short.

29

"Sure. Whether *I* want to. You're indifferent, I take it?"

She braked, looking left and right for a chance to ease into the traffic.

"I'm not indifferent, no. But I get tired of being told that I'm possessive. Telephone me. I'll be free if you want me."

She pulled to the curb in front of a coffee bar. The long lank hair of the girls behind the steamed windows gave them the looks of performers in an underwater ballet. He touched Wanda's mouth with his fingertips and put them to his own mouth. It was a substitute for the kiss he found so hard to give most of the time.

"I'll call you, darling. My regards to the Count."

He slammed the door, waved and ran across the sidewalk. The vaulted garage was bright under sodium lamps. He touched a button outside the deserted office. A bell rang somewhere at the back. An overalled attendant appeared from behind the rows of cars. He moved his head glumly as he recognized Hunter.

"Might have known you'd turn up ternight, didn't I?"

Hunter glanced round the garage. There was no sign of his blue convertible.

"Hello, George. What's that mean — that my battery's flat again?"

The man wiped his hands on a ball of dirty cotton. "Your battery's all right. It's just that I've got you parked awkward. How was it in Russia?"

"Poland," Hunter corrected. "You wouldn't like it, George. The beer's weak and there are no betting shops."

The attendant grunted. "I could do without them, mate. I got done again twice last week. Lumbered on Mr. Rosen's bleedin' certainties. 'E ought stick to making ladies' drawers, not go round tipping 'orses."

He maneuvered the Sunbeam-Alpine from the back row of cars. He wiped the seat and the wheel, giving a vague flourish at the silver horse on the hood.

"There you go, mate. Oil, petrol, water. I checked 'em all meself. Got the life, you 'ave, people like you! Know 'ow long it takes me to get 'ome?"

Hunter nodded. He gave the man a pound note. "An hour and twenty minutes. And your wife snores. You already told me. Is it all right for me to use the phone?"

He went into the office and dialed a Canonbury number. He spoke rapidly.

"Stanley? Hamish Hunter. I've got to see you tonight — no, as soon as possible. It's important."

A mouthful of food seemed to be blocking the reply. "Of course, Hamish. That'll be all right. When and where do you want to meet? I'm just finishing eating."

"The Connaught," said Hunter. "That's about halfway for both of us. Could you leave as you are?"

The voice was dubious. "I don't know about that."

The clock on the wall had no glass. The second hand traveled over a thick film of dust.

"Well as soon as you can," Hunter said impatiently. "If you don't like the idea of the Connaught, somewhere else."

Benstead was mildly amused. "The Connaught's fine. I was thinking about coming as I am, that's all. I happen to be wearing a singlet and a natty pair of long johns. I'll be there in half an hour, OK?"

The garage attendant piloted Hunter into the westbound

traffic. The gauge needles held steady in the right positions. There were cigarettes in the glove compartment, a spray of breath-neutralizer on the ledge over the dash. He gave his mouth a couple of bursts. Benstead missed nothing.

He drove carefully on the wet surface, cutting across Brompton Road, and into the park. The ground beyond the lights stringing the carriageway lay dank and sodden. He was almost at Hyde Park Corner when headlamps in the driving mirror blinded him. He reached up to turn the mirror. Lights from the overtaking vehicle held a glimpse of color behind him. The small red car was twenty yards in his rear, being driven close to the curb.

He braked suddenly, forcing the other car to a halt. It stopped with its front end touching the fender. He climbed over the empty seat, opened the door and walked back to the Mini. Wanda was alone, sitting with her face turned away from him.

"Surprise, surprise," he said. "What's this in aid of?"

She made no answer. He climbed in beside her. The fingers holding her cigarette were shaking violently.

"What are you following me for?" he asked.

She was obstinately silent. He saw that her cheeks were wet and put his arms round her shaking shoulders.

"Wanda," he whispered. "What is it, darling?"

She shook herself free fiercely. "What do you take me for? Someone you can go to bed with and dismiss like a tart?"

The outburst took him by surprise. He stifled the first angry answer.

"Are you out of your mind? I asked you to marry me a couple of hours ago. Or have you forgotten that?"

The movement of her denial was violent. "Of course I

haven't forgotten it. But what would that change — nothing! I've never wanted to dominate your life, in spite of what you think. But at least I thought I'd be part of it. That *sometimes* you'd let me pass the curtain!"

Traffic flashed by. "I want to know why you followed me," he insisted.

She ground her cigarette into the ashtray. Her voice was dull.

"Why? Because I'm a woman, I suppose. I can go off — you don't know where, you don't even care. Because the great Hamish Hunter is *never* jealous. Any woman who even looks at another man must be insane and you've no time for insane people. No place in *your* life for anguish or uncertainty — isn't that right?"

Compassion made him take her in his arms again. He held her tightly, forcing her to listen.

"I want to know one thing, Wanda. Did you really think I was going off with another woman, *did* you?"

She lay in his arms, stiff and unresponsive. "I don't know what I thought, Hamish. All I know is that I'm lost every time you shut me out of your life. You can let me go now. I'm sorry I followed you. I'll never do it again."

He thought for a while, seeking the best way of reassuring her. The problem was too complex.

"Maybe you're right, darling," he said at last. "Maybe everything you say is right but this isn't the time or the place to go into it. I don't want to leave you now — I've *got* to. Do you understand — *got* to!"

Her voice was miserable. "It's this Warsaw thing, isn't it? There's always something to come between us," she said when he nodded.

33

He hitched his shoulders. "This is different. Lives depend on me." He regretted the words as soon as he'd said them. All he needed was bugles blowing the Last Post.

If she noticed she gave no sign. "You won't let me help you?" she asked in a small tight voice.

"Can't, not won't," he corrected gently.

He felt her breath go. She fished in her bag and used her lipstick carefully. When she looked at him again, her face was composed. "Good night, darling."

He stood in the incessant drizzle, watching till the taillamps of the Mini vanished into the swirl at Hyde Park Corner. He walked back slowly to the Sunbeam. She was closer to him than any other woman. What she didn't understand was that the curtain wasn't only lowered on her. At times it was lowered on everyone.

The pavements at each side of Carlos Place were lined with cars. He blinked his lights, catching the attention of the top-hatted doorman. The man recognized the car and shifted a NO PARKING sign, leaving enough space for Hunter to ease in. The hotel bar was a meetingplace for *Quest* staff writers. They drank there, cashed checks, exchanged gossip with publishers, actors and film producers. Hunter left his mac in the car and hurried inside. He stood in the doorway to the bar, lifting a hand as a familiar face came into view. His last meal had been aboard the plane but he needed a drink, not food. He made his way towards the solitary figure seated at the window.

Benstead rose as Hunter neared. The image of a crane was accurate. He stooped from the waist, his large bald head set on bony shoulders. His face was pale brown as if the skin had been too long exposed to hot sun for the color to fade completely. He was wearing a tweed suit and a hand-knitted waistcoat. He clapped Hunter on the shoulder and beckoned a waiter over. Heavy-lidded eyes considered Hunter shrewdly. Voice and manner were just short of pedantic.

"What are you drinking these days?"

"Tomato juice," lied Hunter. He waited till the drinks were on the table and the waiter gone. The only sign of curiosity that Benstead allowed himself was a twitch of white-tufted eyebrows. Hunter lifted his glass. The interview had seemed logical a few short hours ago. Now he was not so sure. Benstead was more than just another newspaperman. As a youngster he'd sailed the Baltic as a radio operator. His wartime activities were never talked about. Since then he had free-lanced, always on the scene when the security checks were toughest — one telephone call ahead of trouble. Those who knew him on Fleet Street respected rather than liked him. Rumor in the same circles had him in the pay of one of the intelligence services.

Hunter trusted him. "I need your help," he said flatly.

Benstead had a long nose, curved like a bird's beak. He tilted his head sideways, eyes lazy under the bushy white brows.

"In trouble with the law again?"

Hunter's jaw muscles tightened. The reference was too recent to be suffered easily. A night's drinking in a pub in Belgravia had been followed by an argument with a cop over a parked car. He'd spent six hours in a police cell. The sequel was best forgotten.

"No," he said carefully. "It's not the law and I'm not pissed. I've never tried to play the cloak-and-dagger game. I wouldn't know where to start. But you do. I've got to talk

35

to someone in authority, Stanley. Someone in Intelligence — and quickly."

Benstead hung in his chair, apparently fascinated by the pattern of the carpet. He lifted his head eventually, smiling mildly.

"There are a lot of stories circulating about me in Fleet Street. Most of them are pretty farfetched."

Voices from the neighboring tables fused to a babble that was punctuated by bursts of shrill laughter. Hunter's chair scraped back.

"You're not talking to *Quest Magazine*. You're talking to *me*. All I want to know is if you're interested. Tell me no and I'll try somewhere else."

Benstead frowned. "You're putting words into my mouth. All I'm saying is that journalists get carried away at times, especially when they gossip. It's an occupational disease. Occasionally I find myself doing it. The truth is, you're as well equipped as I am to get hold of the people you want."

"*Am* I?" said Hunter. "What do I do, phone the Special Branch and give them my name? I'm responsible for people's lives with Sunday the deadline. Do you want to hear any more or not?"

Benstead nodded slowly. Hunter leaned across the table, lowering his voice.

"You know that I've been in Poland?"

Benstead fished a silver snuffbox from his waistcoat pocket. He selected a pastille, closed his teeth on it. He opened his mouth, releasing a strong smell of peppermint.

"I read *Quest*'s advertising. 'The third in a series of brilliant articles exposing the breakdown of Marxist doctrines in Eastern Europe.'" His long-toothed smile robbed the quotation of offense.

Hunter jabbed his hand out. "And don't think that they're *not* breaking down. I saw everything that they wanted me to see in Warsaw. Factories, hospitals, prisons — even a ballet school. OK, so everything looked fine. The people I talked to had no more complaints than the average joe anywhere. Beefs about the price of food and clothes, the difficulties of bringing up kids. The one point they all managed to make was that Communism *worked.* Last night I went back to my hotel room to find a snapshot tucked into the frame of the mirror. A snapshot taken twenty-six years ago of a couple of kids on an ice rink in Switzerland. It was my school and one of the kids was me. The other was a boy called Pawel Poznanski. We roomed together for four years — played on the hockey team. I knew him as well as I've ever known anyone. I went back to Canada shortly after the picture was taken. It was wartime. I never heard of Pawel again."

Benstead's face was sardonic. "I never heard again of anyone I was at school with, Hamish."

Hunter ignored the remark. "I looked round. A note had been put in my pajama pocket. It was typewritten. The initials were P.P. Pawel Poznanski. The message was short.

Be on Wybrzeze Kosciuszkowski at ten o'clock tonight. Make certain you are not followed.

I *wasn't* followed."

Benstead's tongue showed mint fragments. "I don't suppose you were. You're an ingenious bugger when you choose."

"I kept the appointment. Imagine a wide street by the river. Trees in a small park. The cold was too intense for people to loiter. I walked up and down for a quarter of an hour. Suddenly a girl appeared. She knew who I was and spoke to me in English. It was Poznanski's daughter. We started to walk. A cab overtook us and stopped. The driver was her brother. They took me out of the city, northeast to a farmhouse on the edge of a pinewood. A man was waiting there for us."

Benstead scratched the top of his head delicately. "Your friend?"

Hunter's chin lifted. "My friend was arrested by the Security Militia in Cracow at the end of last year. They murdered him in a cell some days afterwards."

Benstead's hooded eyes were intent on Hunter's face. "But the man knew your name?"

Hunter felt the flush creeping up over his collar. "He knew my name, yes. And he knew Poznanski. They had tear sheets there of everything I've written over the past five years. The man's name is Korwin. I've got an idea that it means something in the proper quarters."

Benstead was still attentive. "And that's the story you want to pass on?"

Hunter's fingers tightened round his glass. Benstead's manner was beginning to irritate him.

"It's as much of the story as I'm prepared to tell now."

Benstead took his finger from his nose. "They're not planning to assassinate Gomulka, are they?" he asked drily.

Hunter kept his temper. "*I* know what they're planning to do, Stanley. And if your people have any sense, they'll want to know too. Play it whichever way you like but I want an answer now. Yes or no?"

Benstead emptied his glass. His voice was quiet. "Have you said anything about this to anyone else — anyone at your office?"

Hunter's answer was definite. "Nobody." Whatever he'd said to Wanda was safe enough.

Benstead slipped a pound note under the ashtray. "I'll be back in a moment. I'm going to use the phone."

Hunter watched him walk across the room, angular, bent and awkward. God knows what kept the old boy going — he must be well over sixty. Surely there had to be a bigger spur to living than pigging it alone somewhere in Islington and playing chess against the book. Running around as an intelligence agent's agent was hardly the way to fame or fortune. Benstead was back almost immediately. An old-fashioned ulster with a cape was slung round his shoulders.

"I take it you have your car — then let's go."

They drove west along Mount Street and filtered through the theater-bound traffic into the park. Benstead was sitting bolt-upright in the low seat, munching his pastilles. Hunter wound the window down. The fresh wet air cleared the cloying smell of mint. The lights of the lake-shore restaurant were bright behind washed windows. On the other side of the bridge, darkness hid the squat ugliness of the Armory buildings.

Benstead touched Hunter's knee warningly as the Sunbeam turned into the bend.

"Keep straight ahead!"

Hunter wrenched the wheel, driving onto a broad parking lot that bordered the Serpentine. Summertime saw a hundred cars there, lined up hub to hub. Now there were two, parked thirty yards apart. The soaked grass behind them stretched beyond dripping trees into obscurity.

Hunter cut the lights and motor. The noises of the restaurant drifted across the surface of the lake. He fished a cigarette from the pack and settled back. The other two cars were empty unless the occupants were lying flat on their faces. If he hadn't been sure of the man beside him, he'd have felt tempted to call it a day and go home.

Benstead glanced at his watch for the second time since they had stopped. He reached across the dashboard suddenly and flashed the car's headlamps. He was out of the door before Hunter realized what was happening. He shambled down the path in the direction of the boathouse. Minutes went by. Rain drummed monotonously on the roof. Hunter kept his eyes fixed on the path Benstead had taken. Two men walked into view, under one umbrella. Hunter threw the passenger door open as they neared. The stranger with Benstead climbed in. The older man came round to Hunter's side. He leaned through the window, his face glistening under a soaked hat brim.

"You can talk with complete freedom, Hamish."

He moved away, holding the umbrella high above his head. There was enough light for Hunter to see. The man sitting beside him was about his own age, well built with reddish hair on a foxy head. He wore a tweed jacket, cavalry-twill trousers and Chelsea boots. He smiled, showing strong uneven teeth.

"Let's get down to basics, shall we, Mr. Hunter? You're a journalist and you've just come back from Warsaw — is that right?" The voice was cultured and assured.

Hunter sensed a hint of patronage. His reaction to it was instinctive.

"You've got me at a disadvantage. You know my name — I don't know yours."

The flashed smile was a concession to a point scored. "Smith. I've heard something of your story. I'd like to hear it again from you — from the beginning."

"It's the way I usually tell a story," Hunter said evenly. They were off to a doubtful start.

Smith studied manicured fingers thoughtfully — as if he too had realized it.

"Cut-and-thrust won't get us anywhere, do you think?" he observed mildly. "We'd better start again. You've come back from Poland with some information you want passed on to the right people. You can take it for granted that I know who these are."

Water coursed down the windshield. Hunter touched the wipe switch, clearing arcs that he could see through.

"OK," he said easily. "I went to Warsaw three weeks ago. The last of a series of assignments behind the Iron Curtain for my magazine." He talked for ten minutes, describing and remembering.

Smith's head was clasped in his hands. Occasionally he looked up as if expecting to catch Hunter off guard.

"Very interesting," he said finally. "Your friend's death must have come as a shock to you — the meeting with his children in highly dramatic circumstances."

Hunter turned quickly. Smith's expression was imperturbable. "It was a shock, yes," Hunter agreed.

"How many times did you see this man Korwin?"

"Once. Last night in the farmhouse."

"And he said he was known to the authorities here in London?"

Hunter took his time about answering. *The authorities!* The espionage trade was so bloody security conscious that the mere mention of its function had to be disguised.

"He didn't say that at all. All he said was that he'd be safe once he was in London. *I'm* the one who thought he was a British agent. I still do."

"Describe him to me," said Smith.

Hunter's reconstruction was careful. "On the short side — about five-seven or -eight. Black hair — not too much of it. Dark eyes, some steel teeth and a thin face and body. He might have been anything between thirty-five and forty-five. Difficult to tell."

"And you say that he lisped?"

Hunter pitched his butt through the window. "I didn't say so. But as it happens, he did." The rain was still falling relentlessly. He wondered if Benstead had taken shelter in the restaurant.

Smith was silent for a moment. "Six hundredweight of plastic explosive," he said reflectively. "That would make a large hole anywhere. Difficult to get hold of, I'd have thought, for a man on the run. *And* a silenced submachine gun. He's a resourceful chap, your friend Korwin." His nail tapped on the dashboard. The thin smile was easy to imagine.

The edge to Hunter's patience had been blunted. "Look," he said with meaning. "You're wasting time. Why not have the film read. It's all there?"

"Everything," Smith agreed. He cocked his narrow head. "Right down to call-signs and radio frequencies nobody expects to be used. They're pretty sure of themselves, aren't they?"

Hunter felt his face reddening for the second time that evening.

"They're sure of *you* people. And they've every goddam right to be. Time's running out for them. This country's offered asylum to fiddle players and ballet dancers. It's not too much to expect the same for kids whose father died the way theirs did."

Smith's voice and face were almost too casual. "This would make quite a story for your magazine, wouldn't it?"

Hunter leaned across, spacing his words deliberately. "I hadn't even thought about it. Right now I'm concerned with humanity."

"Nobody doubts that," said Smith. "Have you got the film with you?"

Hunter stared at the outstretched hand. "You didn't expect me to be carrying it around with me, did you?"

Smith lowered his arm. "You talk like a man who's had experience in these matters. Where is it?"

"It's safe enough," said Hunter. It gave him a strange sense of satisfaction that Smith still didn't know *how* he'd brought the film out. "I've had no experience — it's just common sense."

Smith followed a trickle of water down the window with his forefinger.

"Let's go back to this note that was left in your pajamas. Here you were, a chance journalist with a reputation for right-wing sympathies, on an assignment to Warsaw."

"I know it's an unfashionable position to take," Hunter

said suspiciously. "But it's not a criminal offense — not yet, anyway."

Smith fumbled a matchbox from his pocket, looked at the end of a fat cigarette.

"I have no politics. Suppose you lost this film. What would you have done — what were you *told* to do?"

"The question never arose," said Hunter. "And I *haven't* lost it."

Smith leaned back, eyes closed, letting smoke drift from his nostrils.

"You're an intelligent man, Mr. Hunter. Don't you see the basic weakness of your story? You appear in Poland as the representative of a Canadian newsmagazine. You're given the usual treatment — a translator who's certainly a member of the Security Militia — hand-picked interviews — all that sort of thing. Suddenly the tempo livens. You find a snapshot in your hotel room — a note. You're reminded of someone you were at school with twenty-six years ago. There's a mysterious meeting with a stranger. You learn that your school friend is dead and you meet his children. The stranger turns out to be a friend of the dead man, too. And the spark plug of a sabotage team that's going to cripple the Warsaw power system. All very credible on the face of it. The right mixture of action and sacrifice with a touch of humanity thrown in." He opened his eyes and looked at Hunter.

The Canadian canceled his first reply. "With that sort of approach you could make the Gospels sound phony."

Smith's hand waived the point. "All right, I'll put it another way. Imagine yourself on the other side, Mr. Hunter. You want to plant someone in this country — someone with unassailable credentials. You learn that a distinguished foreign journalist has applied for a visa. Everything you can find out about him is favorable to your purpose. So you stage a meeting with him. You expose the details of an important sabotage plot. He comes back to England and tells your story, sold on it, hook-line-and-sinker."

A sudden squall whipped the surface of the lake, lifting the curtain of rain in front of the trees. Benstead was standing under them, looking towards the car. The wind dropped. Rain hid his figure again.

"And what about Poznanski's children?" Hunter asked in a dangerous voice. "Are they part of the scheme, too?"

Smith thought for a moment, smoke curling from his cupped hand. "Makeweight," he decided. "All they do is add the right touch of pathos to the patriotism. They probably don't even know the truth. The thing is that your man is where you wanted him — in West Berlin. Now you pull out all the stops on your organ. Warsaw Radio announces power failures and what is an obvious cover story to account for them. At the same time you leak the clues for your opponents to discover. Now your ploy is complete. You've authenticated a series of nonexistent explosions and planted your man in England with a reputation for derring-do. No, I'm afraid it won't do, Mr. Hunter. The truth is that you've been had."

A nerve started to jump in the skin under Hunter's right eye. He brushed at it impatiently. He chose his words.

"Let me ask you one question, Mr. Smith. Are you the final authority in this affair?"

Smith turned a bland face to him. "Good God, no! I'm nothing more than an assessor of probabilities."

45

Hunter's voice was loud. "Three people, two of them children, are going to risk their lives. Unless you give the signal, they'll be in East Berlin on Sunday, exposed, hunted and with no place to go. At least you'll accept that?"

Smith ground his cigarette end in the ashtray. "They may be in East Berlin. But you can be very sure that they'll not be risking their lives. My advice to you is to go home, have a good dinner and forget all about them. I'm very grateful for the chance to hear all this. It's always a good thing to know the length of the other chap's bowling."

Hunter listened incredulously. "You're standing on your head, man! What is this, some sort of a joke?"

"No joke," Smith said calmly. "Stick to your job, Mr. Hunter, I'm sure you're very good at it."

"You cold-blooded bastard," Hunter said after a while. "You really mean it, don't you?"

Smith leaned across and flashed the headlamps. Benstead appeared in the light. Smith opened the door.

"Leave the worrying to me, Mr. Hunter. Good night."

He was gone before Hunter could answer. He spoke briefly to Benstead, took the umbrella and disappeared into the rain.

Benstead climbed in awkwardly, coat smelling like a wet dog. "What's happened, for God's sake?"

Hunter took a deep breath. "Your friend's just put the spy business back ten years — that's what."

"Will you tell me what happened?" Benstead repeated patiently.

Hunter turned his head. "I've just learned something — that the old crack's true — 'They've got the best spy system in the world in this country — the Russian.' That creep belongs in a museum. There must be *somebody* who'll take me seriously. How do I get to the man in charge, Stanley?"

It was a while before Benstead answered. "You don't. It's as simple as that. You're way out of your depth, Hamish, and you'd better realize it. These people don't exist. Where would you start — the Foreign Office? Nobody would have heard of Smith, of you — you'd be passed from desk to desk till you ran out of time and patience. There *isn't* anyone called Smith. There wasn't even a meeting tonight! Don't you understand that?"

"*You* know there was a meeting — *you* know Smith," Hunter pointed out.

Benstead's face was impassive. "I wouldn't know a thing if you pushed me. Do as he said, forget it."

Hunter switched on the ignition. "I don't forget that easily, Stanley. But don't be alarmed, you won't be involved." He backed out and drove east on the carriageway.

A couple of times he sensed that Benstead was about to say something and thought better of it. Suddenly it came.

"Did you tell Smith you suggested Korwin was a British agent?"

"I did. He knew better," Hunter said curtly.

"And he didn't even want to see the film?"

"Sure he wanted to see it — but not that badly. What was on his mind was the length of the other chap's bowling."

He turned down Park Lane, braking as he saw a cab paying off in front of Aldford House. He bleeped his horn, catching the driver's attention.

"Grab it, Stanley. I'll see you later and thanks, anyway."

Benstead leaned back through the window. "Be kind to

yourself and forget it — the whole thing, Smith included.
You've done your best."

Hunter nodded. Not yet he hadn't, not by a long shot.
"Keep in touch."

He put the car in gear and bulled his way back into the
traffic. The black Ford that had followed him unobserved
was close behind when he stopped on Cockspur Street. The
Quest offices occupied the top floor of a building opposite
Canada House. He unlocked the two doors of the suite.
The acrid stink of Borgerund's cigars persisted in spite of the
air-conditioning.

He looked through the glass partition into the switchboard room. There was nobody in the place. It was Kramer's
turn for the night watch. He'd probably slipped out for
something to eat. Hunter pushed the swing door. Home
addresses and phone numbers of everyone working in the
bureau were on a board by the telephone operator's desk. He
found the number of the staff photographer and dialed. The
answering voice was sleepy. Hunter perched himself on the
edge of the desk

"Gerry? This is Hamish. Look — I want a job done —
a personal job. Nobody else in the bureau must know about
it. How long would it take you to blow up some pieces of
microfilm?"

The phone went dead. A hand was covering the mouthpiece at the other end. The photographer came on again.

"Do I have to develop or is it a print?"

"Prints," said Hunter. "I'm sure about that. I don't know
the millimeter size or whatever you call it. There are four
pieces. Each is about a quarter-inch square."

"I can show you the blow-up on a screen immediately. It'll take half an hour if you want legible copies. OK?"

"Could you do it tonight?" said Hunter. "I can bring them over to your place right away."

The man made a sound of despair. "Have a heart, Hamish. This is my first evening home in two weeks and I'm not alone. Won't tomorrow do?"

Hunter lifted his rear from the desk. "Tomorrow morning, then. First thing. I'll meet you here at Cockspur Street, ten o'clock. And keep it under your hat."

He hung up and reconnected the switchboard to the answering service. He'd need Wanda to translate the message. He could reach her at any time. His main problem was getting hold of a radio ham who could be trusted. A man with the necessary equipment. Maybe Benstead could help. But how far he could be trusted now was something else again. Duty or whatever it was that fueled him might send him straight to Smith with the news. The Telex machine clattered before he could give the problem more thought. He stood over the table, holding the strip in his fingers as it came out of the feeder.

Toronto x Head Office x have recvd no answr tlx of 13–15 hrs today x is hunter back x signed Dunnxxxxxxxx

The machine went dead. He tore off the strip and took it into the main office. Kramer's desk light was on. Hunter used it to pin down the Telex message and scribbled a note.

Tell Toronto I'm back. H.H.

His own office was in darkness. He switched on the lamps. There was a vase with red roses on his desk next to Wanda's portrait. He opened the drawer mechanically, feeling for the

49

bottle of scotch he kept there. Someone had moved it. He smiled in spite of himself. That would be Ginny, preserving his image for the cleaning woman. She was beginning to be as much governess as secretary. She worried about everything — his drinking habits, the length of his hair and the buttons on his shirt. She made it plain that she wasn't too high on Wanda's care of him. He put out the light, locked up and went down to his car.

The fountains behind Canada House played on a dark empty square. Rain-blurred lights blinked on and off at the end of the Strand. The traffic was still heavy. He took the fast route home, down the Mall and along Buckingham Palace Road. He made a right turn at the Albert Bridge onto the Embankment. A hundred yards on, a car overtook him. It swung in sharply, forcing the Sunbeam over. He braked hard, swearing as he felt the front wheel hit the curb. Doors slammed in the car in front. Two men ran back, one to each side of the stalled Sunbeam.

Hunter shoved his head through the open window. "What the hell is this — are you guys trying to wreck me?"

The man's face was thin and spectacled under a cloth cap. "Police officers," he said sharply. "Let's see your driving license."

The man's partner opened the passenger door as Hunter leaned forward to look in the glove compartment. The Canadian swung round belligerently. Something hit him hard at the base of the skull. The force of the blow pitched him on his face. He lay there, sprawled across the seat. He was stunned yet conscious that hands were going through his pockets. He heard the breathing of the man who was holding his shoulders down — the noise of water running in the gutter. He opened his eyes as he was turned over roughly. All he could see was the gloved hand that caught his mouth and chin, forcing his head up. Fingers explored the lining of his jacket, ripped his tie from his collar.

The two men were gone as quickly as they had come. He pulled himself up in time to see the car drive off, lights extinguished. The episode had taken three minutes at the most. Outside wind and rain blew on an empty stretch of sidewalk. There were no witnesses. Apart from the opening sentence, neither man had uttered a word. He touched the back of his neck tenderly. There was no swelling — just a dull ache. He started picking up the contents of his pocket from the floor. Wallet, press cards, keys. Nothing had been taken.

He left his collar undone and put his tie in his pocket. He'd been expertly sapped and searched, but for what? He had no enemies, no gambling debts. If he went to the police, all they'd do would be listen, wipe his nose and send him home with a nickel clutched in his fist. Smith's face suddenly was vivid in his mind's eye, cunning and remote. The assault had to be something to do with Smith. There could be no other answer. He drove the last half-mile shakily, an eye on the driving mirror. He let himself into the apartment building and stood for a while in the entrance hall, listening. The music had stopped in the flat opposite. Plummer's lights were out. Furniture was being dragged across the floor somewhere overhead. Voices of a man and woman were loud in argument. The Fanshawes' rearrangement of house was a weekly occurrence.

He shut his own door and leaned against it. The wall mirror glimmered, the reflection showing a lighter patch at the end of the hall. He turned round slowly. His bedroom door was half open. He'd left it closed — he was sure of it.

"Wanda!" he said sharply. He moved cautiously into the bedroom, throwing the light switch as he passed. The bed was as he had left it, the curtained windows shut. Water was dripping in the bathroom. He walked over to the dresser. At first glance nothing appeared to have been moved. Photographs, hairbrushes, electric razor, the pinch-bottle half filled with sixpences — all were in their usual places.

He carried the bottle to the bed and emptied a shower of silver on the sheet. He sorted through them hurriedly, flipping the coins over, looking for the date of minting. The two pieces he wanted were still there. He unscrewed them, staring down at the squares of microfilm. He ran into the sitting room. His books and papers were undisturbed. He opened his briefcase. Everything was there — passport, flight vouchers, traveler's checks. But instinct told him someone had been in the flat since he had left.

He dragged the curtains across the windows and sat down at the table, the opened coins in front of him. They'd mugged him and searched his flat. Whoever *they* were, this was what they were looking for. What *Smith* was looking for. Who else could pull a caper like this, putting himself above the law? In any case, nobody but Smith and Benstead knew about the film. Smith had been bluffing and the reason was obvious. The disbelief was a cloak for something far more sinister.

Smith believed the story, all right, but he didn't want Korwin. The Pole was a dead member, exposed and useless. And Poznanski's children were of no concern to a professional intelligence outfit. No, they wanted the sabotage and that was all. There would be no pick-up in Potsdam. Just Korwin, the boy and the girl waiting for the help that would never come. Smith's headache was the film. As long as it wasn't in his possession, he could never be sure that Korwin wouldn't be warned off in time.

Smith's next move was anyone's guess. He invented the rules as he went. Hunter considered the telephone. He could call the police — dial 999 and say what? Benstead was right. If he took his complaint to the authorities, he'd get a runaround that could last months. Whatever he did had to be done by himself. The essential was speed. The first thing to do was plant the film somewhere where it would be safe.

He levered the small square of film out with a matchstick and screwed the coins together again. The film he sealed in an envelope and addressed it to himself. There was no one in the cottage. The letter would get there sometime tomorrow. He'd have it at Gerry's by the evening — make sure the photographer had his equipment ready. In the meanwhile, he'd have to think of a way of sending the signal.

He opened the back door cautiously. Rain lashed the short length of the passage leading out to the Embankment. He ran as far as the mailbox and dropped the letter through the slot. A car swished by, spraying the sidewalk with mud. The only person in sight was a man holding an umbrella over a small dog. He closed the back door and bolted it. The beer in the refrigerator was cold. He fished out a can, punctured it and strained the icy tang through his teeth. He carried the can into the living room. There was one thing Smith had forgotten — the power of public opinion.

He stood for a while, concealed behind the curtains. A

vista of washed buildings showed beyond the triangle of grass. The lone tree swayed in the rising wind. He cleared space on the table and fed a sheet of paper into his typewriter. The piece had to be carefully written with no names or countries mentioned. It must be an appeal for political sense rather than a tearjerker. He was sanguine about getting the right sort of article past a D-notice. The film would be evidence that he was neither fool nor liar. Ideas came slowly. He set the table with scotch and beer and concentrated. After a while he caught fire, composing his outline fluently. He banged out a thousand words and read them back, yawning. It was OK but the note was too serious. As Smith would say, too crusading. He needed something lighter — a satirical treatment that would provoke thought behind the grin of the reader. He poured himself more scotch, realizing that the liquor was getting its work in. His mind jumped from alcohol to Wanda. He pulled himself up, crossed the room and took the phone. A clipped voice answered his call.

"Yampolski."

Hunter aimed his rear at the nearest chair, still holding the phone.

"It's Hamish Hunter. Is Wanda there?" He held the receiver well away from his ear. The Count addressed the telephone like a troop of cavalrymen.

"She is not here, no. *Who* is spikking?"

"Hamish Hunter," he repeated. "Have you an idea when she's likely to be back, sir?"

"Ah, Hemmish! Comment ça va, mon vieux?" After twenty-two years in the country, Wanda's father still affected defeat by the English language. The pose allowed use of his perfect French — a language, he explained, that was second

54

to all members of the Polish aristocracy. "Ma fille est sortie."

Hunter blocked a hiccough. "Thanks. And you've no idea when she'll be back?"

The reply was faintly satisfied. "Absolument pas, mon cher. Vous allez m'excuser. Je dois moi-même sortir. A bientôt!"

Hunter cradled the phone. He looked at his watch, amazed that it was no more than ten o'clock. She'd probably gone to the movies. The thought left him with a sense of injustice. Typical that the moment he needed her, she found something better to do. He wanted to talk — to be heard by someone who'd believe what he said. He sat down at the typewriter again, working over the new draft. From time to time he fixed himself a drink, chasing neat scotch with beer till he could no longer see the keyboard clearly. He read the piece through, stretched and staggered out to the kitchen. The haddock was where he had left it in the saucepan. He was no longer hungry. The empty vodka bottle caught his eye. He lifted it from the table and smashed it on the floor. He stood for a while looking at the broken shards, then swept them onto a newspaper. He felt his way along the hall, shedding his clothes as he went. By the time he reached the bed he was down to his underpants. He let them fall round his ankles, stepping out with one foot. He aimed the pants with the other, lurching as they sailed through the air to the chair.

He lowered himself carefully onto the bed and rolled between the sheets. He shut his eyes tight, waiting for the room to stop spinning. Somewhere in his fogged brain he heard the phone ringing. How much later he couldn't tell. There was no past or future, nothing but the present. An enveloping darkness into which he sank gratefully.

Wanda Yampolska

21 February 1967

23 BELL STREET was a narrow structure wedged into a row
of larger houses. Weather and grime had touched the brick-
work with the color of old rust. The paint on the outside
window sashes had blistered and burst, exposing the raw
wood beneath. From the top floor there was a distant view of
Chelsea Football Ground. Five days a week the flower ped-
dler's cart was parked in front of the house. The walls at the
back enclosed a few square yards of muddy earth over which
rain spouted from the broken guttering. She had lived in
the house ever since she remembered.

She turned away from the window. Her father's bedroom
and her own were on the second floor. A door in the staircase outside divided the house in two. A reticent Polish bach-
elor occupied the upper half — an ex-professor of mathe-
matics now employed as a Tote operator. She folded a green
silk scarf lengthways and tied her hair behind her ears. The
room was her refuge. A spring lock on the door ensured absolute privacy. She did her own cleaning. Flame-colored
curtains and carpet gave the room warmth. Bed, dresser
and clothes closet were Danish-designed and in light pine.
Her books were in a case by the window. Back copies of *Quest*

were piled on a prayer stool. She finished making up, leaving the hand mirror by the velvet-and-silver frame. The portrait of her mother had been taken fifteen years ago, shortly before her death.

She went out on the landing, sniffing the sweet vegetable smell permeating the house. Most evenings, her father prepared himself a meal of Polish sausage and beetroot soup. It had been a long time since they had eaten in the house together. She went down the stairs slowly, passing the photograph of the Count in the waisted uniform of a military cadet. The Count measuring the tusks of a wild boar. The Count and Countess walking the deck of a yacht in dated summer clothing. The Count again, peering from the turret of a tank against the background of North African desert.

She halted suddenly, gripping the banister rail. The mirror in the hall reflected the scene in the room opposite. Her father was leaning over the dining table — a slim wiry figure in a well-cut dinner jacket. His hair was completely white, brushed back in long wings over small flat ears. She watched him extract the wallet from her bag, screwing a monocle into his right eye, the better to assess its contents. He took out two pound notes and concealed them between the pages of a magazine.

The kernel of contempt had been too long in her mind for her to be affected. She had hated her father ever since she could remember. She hated his public arrogance and private pettiness — his loose-mouthed friends who pinched her teen-age bottom with avuncular freedom. Secretly, she hated everything her father stood for — the sham and dishonesty of his false patriotism. Her choice had been deliberate — she lived with a man she neither loved nor respected so that

57

she could profit from the things he stood for. She had gone straight from school to *Le Cercle Polonais* as committee secretary. That was nine years ago. Her office was the nerve center of an émigré society still clinging stubbornly to its own traditions. Through it came the stream of begging letters, the wild denunciations, the Pan-Polish organizations as far away as Australia and the Argentine. Her background and position were invaluable to her cause.

She waited till her father was back in his favorite position. He stood, erect in front of the coal fire, surveying the shabby comfort of the room as if surprised to find himself in such surroundings. She stood in the doorway, addressing him in the formal Polish he insisted she use in the house.

"Dobry wieczór, papo! I am going out."

He hooked the monocle from his breast pocket again. A thread of colored ribbon ran through his lapel. His smile revealed teeth too perfect to be natural.

" 'Good evening, papa, I am going out!' " he mimicked. "What daughterly devotion! May I ask where?"

She picked up her handbag, putting it down again deliberately on top of the magazine hiding the two pound notes. She adjusted her scarf in the mirror. The scene was a familiar one. Each petty theft was followed by an attack on her — as if her father found it compulsive to justify himself.

She spoke over her shoulder. "Nowhere in particular. Just out."

Count Yampolski waved his hand elegantly. "Then, good night! If you intend to be late I shall not be here. I have business to attend to in Knightsbridge." The eye behind the monocle flickered as she picked up her handbag.

She looked at him, hiding her scorn. Her father's routine

was no secret. He called first at his bridge club. There'd be the gracious exchange of greetings as he searched the room for a likely face — a victim for one of the crooked chemmy games that paid him a commission. If he had no luck there, he'd try one of the neighboring hotels. Some time after three, he would come back to Bell Street and sleep till late morning.

She touched her lips to his cheek, smelling the expensive scent he used habitually. The chances were that it had been bought with her money.

"Good night, father."

"You are seeing Hemmish, perhaps?" he asked.

"I am not seeing Hamish," she replied steadily.

His eyes were bright with malice. "You are twenty-seven years old. Men weary of devotion but only after they have experienced it. Remember your father's advice."

She slammed the street door on the sound of his laughter. She drove to South Kensington and found a parking place at the bottom of Queen's Gate. She sat for a while in the car, watching the broad thoroughfare. People were getting out of a cab in front of a nearby hotel. A man crossed the street, holding his hat firmly as the rising wind threatened it. The low sky overhead was menacing.

She locked the car and walked quickly along Harrington Gardens, looking straight in front of her. The mechanics of evasion had become second nature. She used shop windows as mirrors, street crossings as vantage points. She hurried into the subway station and bought a ticket for two stops up the line. She boarded the first train in, standing near the exit doors. As they started to slide shut, she stepped back on the platform. The negress in L.P.T.B. uniform watched indifferently as Wanda ran into a tunnel marked NO ENTRY. She pushed her way past the crowd coming from the opposite direction, climbed the bridge and boarded a westbound train. The coach was full. She stood, swaying from the strap as far as Earl's Court Road. She rode the elevator up to street level, certain that she had not been followed.

A group of youths loitered in the station entrance, their cheap gaudy clothing a foil for matted shoulder-length hair. The oneway traffic hurtled south showering the pedestrians with slush. For the most part these were Negroes, Hindus or Pakistanis. A torn sticker wrapped round a lamppost said KEEP BRITAIN WHITE!

She hurried across the street as the signals changed. She turned left through a narrow passage, emerging two blocks from the station. She walked straight into the delicatessen store across the street. Giant hams and sausages hung from hooks. The shelves were stacked with cans bearing Polish labels. She waited till the store was empty, pretending an interest in the cheese tray. The white-coated man behind the counter jerked his head. She went through the door at his back. The stuffy room was used as office and storeroom. Cartons of food were piled on top of one another. A man rose from the chair by the gas fire. He was sharp-featured with an inch-wide strip of black beard that followed his jawline. He wore heavy square spectacles under a short bristle of hair. He lifted her hand to his lips.

"You are late," he reproved in Polish.

She sat down, making a lap for her handbag and smoothing her coat behind her knees.

"It was unavoidable. I am sorry."

He wore a flower in the lapel of his camel's hair jacket. He lit a cigarette, his voice courteous.

"The Bayswater number is reserved for emergencies. You know this of course."

She looked at him steadily. "This *is* an emergency." A canary in a cage hanging from the ceiling cheeped twice and lapsed into silence. She spread her hands, watching his expression. "Hunter is back. He returned from Warsaw this afternoon."

The cigarette holder bobbed in the Pole's mouth. "This is not news. I have full information about his visit."

She touched the back of her hair, lifting it from her neck. "I wouldn't be too sure about that. It is possible that your information could be incomplete. Does the name Korwin have any significance for you?"

His tone was sharp. "Korwin? Where did you hear this name — in what context?"

The canary scattered seed into her lap. She brushed it off her coat.

"From Hunter, this afternoon. It's someone he saw in Warsaw — clandestinely. He's been on edge ever since I met him at the airport — dropping mysterious hints — things like he's doing more for Poland than my father has ever done. You know his politics. That's why I telephoned."

He took off his spectacles and looked at her with black, dilated pupils. He wiped his eyes with his handkerchief.

"Tell me what he said, everything."

He heard her out, smoking as he walked. Finally he turned, jabbing the cigarette holder in her direction.

"You returned to his apartment with him. How did he

61

act there? Did you have the impression that he might have been hiding something — I mean something in his apartment? Did he show any signs of nervousness?"

She thought back and shook her head. "He was nervous, yes, but not in that way. I saw what he had in his bag and briefcase. It was exactly what he'd taken with him. The only thing I hadn't seen before was a snapshot. He left it out quite openly, on top of his dresser. It was a picture of two boys. He was one of them. There were two names on the back. Hunter's and a Polish name — Poznanski."

Someone had gummed newspaper over the panes of the window. He glanced towards it as he spoke.

"*Pawel* Poznanski?"

She moved her head in agreement. "That's right."

He came closer to her, like a hypnotist going into his act. "I told Warsaw that Hunter was dangerous. I told them when he first applied for a visa. They chose to ignore me. The names you have mentioned prove that he's dangerous. One of them is dead — Poznanski. Korwin is an *alias* of a man wanted by the *Bezpieka* — a fascist criminal. Both men were enemies of the state. You have done well, Yampolska. Your cooperation has been invaluable."

The stuffy room smelled of cheese and, inevitably, mice. She sneezed hard into her handkerchief. It was the only recognition she had had since her first brash move eight years ago. She'd been nineteen and in Paris. She had walked into the Polish Embassy, introduced herself and said what she wanted. An elderly man had given her coffee, a cigarette and a polite refusal. Three years went by before anyone contacted her again. Since then she had worked for them consistently.

"I have done my duty," she said quietly.

He inclined his head. "We are not ungrateful. Do you have access to Hunter's apartment?"

"I have a key." It was time to make her admission. "I followed him this evening, after we had parted. He collected his car. I thought I should know where he went."

The words hung for a moment. His forehead creased. "And what happened?"

She moved her shoulders elegantly. "I was careless. He saw my car in his driving mirror. He stopped. He wanted to know why I was following him. I played the jealous woman. It went off well enough. He believed me. He always does."

Light glinted from the tinted lens as he tilted his head. "Are you an ambitious woman, Yampolska?"

She treated the question seriously. "Ambitious in what way, Adam?"

He lowered his voice. "Korwin is a dagger at the throat of our country. Whoever traps him is sure of advancement in the Party. It could be us."

She had known him for two years. It was the first time he had ever dropped the mask of selfless dedication. The thought that she was responsible excited her. She suddenly felt important.

He started walking again, talking as he went. "This man Korwin has a long history of sedition and sabotage. A mad dog of a man, Yampolska, and highly dangerous. If he met Hunter it was for good reason. I am convinced that we have no time to waste. I suspect that Hunter has been given some message and told to contact the British Intelligence. You say you have a key. Can you use it at any time?"

She twisted the ring on her finger uncertainly. "I don't know. He comes and goes without warning."

He sat down, covering his eyes with his hand like a man praying. He took them away after a moment and snapped his fingers.

"His apartment will have to be searched — but not by you. Where is your car?"

"Queen's Gate." She needed fresh air. The heat in the room was overpowering.

He spoke quickly, "There's a chemist's shop at the corner of Fulham Road and Drycott Gardens. Go there on your way home and ask for Mr. Berendt. He'll give you a pill. It's quite small, no more than three grains. You must give this to Hunter in some form of drink, tonight. Do you think you can do that? The drug is completely tasteless. It is effective within ten minutes."

"I don't know what time he'll be home," she said doubtfully. "But I'll go there anyway. I'll think of an excuse."

He glanced at his watch. "Ten minutes should give you an ample margin of safety. The moment you're sure he's unconscious, call the Bayswater number. There'll be someone there all the time. And no private telephones, remember. A booth. Locate one before you go to the apartment."

"And you don't want me to look for anything — papers?"

He draped a military-style raincoat round his shoulders. "You wouldn't know what to look for. Listen to what he says and forget nothing. I am depending on you, Yampolska. There must be complete trust between us if we are to succeed."

The solemnity in his voice impressed her. Her eyes promised what he needed. Had he told her the pill was arsenic, she'd have given it blindly to Hunter.

He lifted her hand to his lips and left the room. She waited for the prescribed ten minutes. The man in the store was stacking cans on the shelves. He turned his back deliberately as she passed through.

The chemist's shop was in the new British fashion. Showcases crammed with toilet articles, hot-water bottles, dog collars and leashes occupied most of the space. She walked to the end of the shop. A sign over the counter read:

PHARMACEUTICAL DEPARTMENT

An elderly man in a white coat was filling a prescription. She glanced round the shop. No one was there but the two of them.

"Mr. Berendt?"

He went on pouring liquid into a bottle. For a moment she thought that he had not heard. He corked the bottle and stuck a label on it. He opened a drawer and placed an envelope on the counter. She hesitated, purse in hand. He shook his head and vanished behind a partition.

The church clock on the corner of Redclyffe Gardens was striking eleven as she opened her street door. Her father was sitting in front of a tray in the living room. He wiped his mouth with a napkin as she passed and called up the stairs after her.

"Your *sortie* must have been boring. You are home early. Hemmish will be reassured. He telephoned. I said I had no idea when you would be back."

65

She did her best to make her voice normal. "Oh really? Where was he?"

Her father came out to the hall. "At home as far as I could make out." He covered his throat with a white silk scarf and put on a black overcoat.

She looked down over the banisters. "Did he say what he wanted?"

Her father's smile was sardonic. "If he did, I didn't understand him. If you intend to go there I suggest a liter of strong coffee."

She ran up the stairs to her bedroom. She switched on the light and looked round. Just a year ago he'd had a key made to fit her door. She'd had the lock changed twice since then. She tore open the envelope. The pill was enclosed in a plastic capsule.

The street door below was slammed violently. Window frames were still rattling as she came out to the landing. The hall lights were off. She ran down, carried the phone to the glow of the fire and dialed Hunter's number. It rang without answer. She gave her father time to find a cab. With money in his pocket he would never use a bus. He had gone when she ventured out on the street.

The pavements were drying in the wind. People streamed from the Forum Cinema as the traffic signals held her. She forked right towards Chelsea. A couple of cars were parked in front of Blake House. Hunter's Sunbeam was one of them. She drove her own car alongside. The curtains in his flat were drawn. There was no sign of light. She climbed out, clutching her handbag tightly to her chest. The entrance doors swung open as she neared. A man emerged, trapped in the radiance from the sign over the portico. He was tall with stooped shoulders. His arms were hidden under a caped ulster. It was too late for her to turn back. They looked one another full in the face. He smiled, inspecting her from under stiff white brows. She hesitated momentarily, glancing beyond him into the hall. She knew all the tenants in the block by sight. This man she had never seen before. He was still holding the door open. She passed him and walked up the stairs on impulse. The landing on the second story was dim. She stood at the window, peering down into the forecourt. The stranger was walking away in the direction of King's Road.

She tiptoed back down to the hall. People were still moving about upstairs. The man might have come from any one of four apartments. There was a pungent smell that reminded her of a dentist's surgery — or was it toothpaste. Suddenly she had it. *Peppermint.* She raised the flap of Hunter's mailbox and put her ear to it. A rasping noise came from the bedroom. It was a moment before she identified the sound as Hunter's breathing. She put her key in the lock and turned gently. The door swung open. The bedroom door was ajar. Enough light came from the electric heater to see the clothes strewn over the floor. Hunter was lying on his back, partially covered with a sheet. His mouth was wide.

She stepped across his trousers into the living room. Her feet made no sound on the carpet. She felt her way across the room to the angle lamp and thumbed the button. Hunter had been working. A thin sheaf of typescript lay beside his machine. She bent over the table, reading the top sheet. The title was in caps.

The first few paragraphs made no sense. A noise in the

hall sent her fingers flying to her mouth. She whirled round. Hunter stumbled into the room, clutching his tartan rug round his middle. A plume of gray-brown hair rose from the back of his head. He hung onto the door handle, swaying as he looked at her.

"It's gone midnight, for God's sake! What kept you so long?"

She watched him carefully, her heart hammering. His voice was slow and slurred, his eyes fogged.

"I went to the Guild," she said quickly. "I didn't get back till after eleven. Daddy told me you'd phoned. What is it, Hamish — what's the matter?"

He lowered himself into a chair. "Get me a drink. I've got to think."

There was one full can of beer left on the table. She gave it to him. He punctured it, drank and wiped his mouth on the back of his hand.

"Do you love me?" he asked flatly.

She looked down at him, shaking her head, "Of course I love you. Sometimes I wonder why."

He pulled her down on his knees. "Listen, Wanda. You've got to help me. I wasn't kidding this afternoon. I'm sitting on a time bomb with three people's lives depending on me."

She took his face in her hands, searching his eyes. "It's something to do with Korwin, isn't it?"

He moved his head impatiently. "Sure it's Korwin. Unless I stop it, something's coming off on Sunday that will stand the Polish People's Republic on its ear. And I've *got* to stop it. Nobody here wants any part of the deal."

She felt as if she were on the edge of a frozen pond, forced to go forward and not knowing how thick the ice was.

"But what deal, darling? What is it that's going to happen?"

He gripped her tightly by the elbows, his voice slurred. "You don't have to know. I don't want you running risks. I was stopped and mugged tonight — five hundred yards away from the flat. Two men in a car. And the place had been searched. They missed what they were looking for. They'll probably try again."

He turned his head suddenly. She followed the direction of his glance. All she saw was a couple of coins in an ashtray on the table.

"You can't *do* this to me, Hamish," she reasoned. "Who attacked you, who searched the flat? If you're in trouble I have the right to know about it."

His body stiffened. "There you go with your 'rights' again! You've got to help me without asking questions. You'll know soon enough. I want something translated from Polish into English. Can you think of anyone with a shortwave sender — someone you can trust?"

She slipped from his lap. "A shortwave sender? I don't know. I'd have to think."

She picked the two sixpenny pieces from the glass ashtray, the gesture casual. His eyes flickered. She put the coins down again. Something about them bothered him, that much was certain.

"Go to bed, darling," she urged. "If you don't sleep you'll be good for nothing."

He got up unsteadily. She helped him into the bedroom and tucked him in. She tore the pill from its wrapping, watching him through a crack in the bathroom door. The pill disintegrated immediately, leaving the water unclouded. She dropped a couple of seltzer tablets in the glass and took it through to him. He opened his eyes as she neared the bed.

"Drink this, darling. It'll do you good."

She watched him drain the glass and cough. He rolled over on one side. She rinsed the glass under the hot water faucet. There was no trace of sediment. She came back and sat at the foot of the bed. His face had gone slightly red. He was breathing heavily through a slack mouth. She kept her eyes on her watch. Ten minutes passed. She pulled the sheet back, exposing his body. He was lying on one hip again. She pinched the skin over his kidneys with thumb and forefinger. She left weals in the flesh but he lay quite still. She lifted one of his eyelids. The pupil had rolled and was staring at the ceiling. She re-covered him with the sheet and let herself out of the apartment.

The nearest telephone was a hundred yards away, at the foot of the bridge, facing Oakley Street. She hurried towards it, keeping close to the stone parapet bordering the river. Fifteen feet below, on the other side, water sucked and gurgled in the darkness. The two booths were unoccupied. She rang the Bayswater number. As soon as the receiver was lifted she used the code greeting. Adam answered. It was hard to keep the triumph from her voice.

"I have done it. He is in bed."

She heard him speak to someone in the room. A door slammed. Then he was back.

"Is there another way out of the building?"

"Through the kitchen." A muffled figure was crossing the bridge. Without knowing why she thought of the stranger she had met outside Blake House. "There's a passage leading to the Embankment," she added.

"Listen to me carefully. Go back immediately. Dress Hunter and turn all the lights off. Then open the kitchen door and wait."

"Dress him in what?" she asked hurriedly.

"The clothes he was wearing. I'm sending two men. Do whatever they say." He was off the line before she could tell him about the coins.

A few lights still showed on the top floor of Blake House. Other than that the building was in darkness. She slipped back into the apartment. Hunter was lying exactly as she had left him. A dribble of spit had run from the corner of his mouth onto the pillow. She collected his clothing and dragged him upright in the bed. His head rolled helplessly. She pulled his underpants on and buttoned his shirt. Getting his trousers over his knees was more difficult. Next came his jacket. Knotting his tie gave her more trouble. She fastened his shoes, remembering the double loops he made in the laces. She stepped back, looking at him with disgust.

It was three years since they had met at a party. He'd never known that she'd gone there under orders, specially to meet him. Since then he had served her purpose, his tongue loosened by drink and conceit. For the last eighteen months she had been his mistress. Her mind refused the term "lover," recalling the icy hatred with which she surrendered her body.

She went out to the kitchen and unfastened the bolts on the back door. The key turned stiffly in the heavy mortise lock. She pushed the door open wide. A faint light shone down the passage, coming from the street lamps along the Embankment. The kitchen clock showed twenty-five minutes after midnight. She dragged a chair to the table and sat facing the passage. It was over with Hunter — it *had* to be over.

71

The thought excited her. With Adam as an ally, she might even be used in Poland. His words had hinted as much. She lit one cigarette after another, stubbing out each, half smoked.

Minutes passed without anything happening. Suddenly she heard movement at the end of the passage. Shadows passed the windows. The two men were in the kitchen before she reached the door. One of them closed and bolted it. The other spoke in Polish.

"No lights — whisper. Where is he?"

Both men were dressed in dark clothing. One stank of wine. She led the way into the bedroom. Now she could see their faces. One had round smooth cheeks slashed with a knife-scar. The other wore a thin black mustache. Both had the same look of implacability. The scar-faced man had a gun in his left hand. He bent over Hunter and looked up sharply.

"When did you give him the pill?"

She looked at her watch, wondering why her hand had begun to tremble.

"Nearly an hour ago."

She heard the second man in the hall, trying the front door. His companion dropped the gun in his overcoat pocket.

"Where are his papers — his passport?"

She pointed at the dresser. The man with a mustache readied a mini-camera. His partner held up Hunter's passport. She jumped as a flashbulb filled the room with brilliance. Bulbs exploded in quick succession as each page of the passport was photographed. The scar-faced Pole took the gun from his pocket again. He seemed happier with it in his hand. He motioned her into the sitting room. The other man's flashlight found the sheaf of typescript on the table.

He hesitated, then used his camera on it. He pocketed the spent bulbs and empty film packs. The beam from the flash took Wanda full in the face.

"Is there a maid — someone who cleans?"

She shielded her eyes with her hand. "Only on Monday and Thursday — from two till four in the afternoon."

The light was removed from her face. "We are coming back in the morning. There is no more time tonight. Give me the key to the apartment."

She opened her bag obediently. The two men walked back into the bedroom, leaving her alone. She picked up the two sixpenny pieces and dropped them in her purse on impulse. A noise in the hall turned her head. The scar-faced man was in the doorway.

"Bring your car round to the end of the passage."

She let herself out through the front door. The building was quiet. She hurried across the forecourt, pursued by the tapping of her own feet. The motor caught first time, roaring as she fed it too much gas. She reversed out of the parking lot, watching the upper windows nervously. She circled the block and stopped at the mouth of the alley. She fished automatically for a cigarette. The rain had stopped. Staggered lamps lit the sweep of the deserted road. Footsteps shuffled along the passage. The Poles appeared, carrying Hunter between them. She pulled the door-catch hastily. They heaved Hunter into the back of the car. The man with the mustache followed. His partner climbed in beside her.

"Straight ahead and drive carefully."

The gun was in his lap. She put the car in gear. She could see Hunter in the driving mirror, propped upright in the corner. She neither knew nor cared what these men were going to do with him. Whatever Adam's plan was, it would take care of her safety. Her pilot's instructions were precise. They drove across Vauxhall Bridge Road, following the Embankment, past Millbank and the Houses of Parliament and on to Charing Cross. Here the Pole sent her left onto a short street running down from the Strand. A row of houses faced a church. She halted in front of it. The two men moved in swift unison, dragging Hunter across the sidewalk into the churchyard. One of them daubed the Canadian's knees with mud and unzipped the front of his trousers. They laid him out on the steps of the porch and ran back to the car. The man beside her spoke briefly. She gunned to the top of the street, parked and entered a phone booth. Her call was answered immediately.

"Information Room, New Scotland Yard. May I help you?"

Her voice was shrill with indignation. "There's a drunken man in the churchyard of St. Luke's, Adelphi Terrace. He's been there for at least half an hour, behaving scandalously. No, I *don't* see a police officer in the area. I insist on something being done, immediately."

The two men watched her narrowly as she came back to the car.

"They're sending someone," she said. They sat in silence as the minutes passed. Suddenly the street was filled with the double note of a police alarm. A patrol wagon careered past the parked car and skidded to the curb in front of the church. Two uniformed constables pounded into the yard. They reappeared, seconds later, carrying Hunter by the feet and shoulders. They bundled him onto the back of the wagon. The driver made a U turn and shot by, his alarm still going.

The man sitting beside her smiled for the first time. "Efficiency. I like. Drive on."

She crossed the Strand and headed north. The sliver of mirror showed the man behind slumped sideways, head on chest as if asleep. Once he stretched, yawning as a police car flashed by traveling in the opposite direction. Her pilot looked straight in front of him, arms folded. His instructions were no longer necessary. She already knew where she was going. Past Baker Street she turned onto the Outer Circle, then left, changing down at the foot of the long incline. A half-mile up, her guide cleared a space on his window with a gloved hand.

"Down here."

She wheeled onto the quiet avenue. Skeletal trees whipped in the wind. Her headlamps stared down a gentle slope. A pair of gates gapped the wall on their left. A board glimmered in the bushes.

THE FRIENDSHIP PRESS

(A non-profit organization supported by voluntary contributions)

She swung the Mini through the entrance and stopped at the end of the graveled driveway. It was months since she had been here. She followed the men down a path screened by dense laurel. The back door was open. Inside, the narrow passage ended with a pair of steps. She pushed a second door, standing blinking in the glare from powerful overhead lamps. The lock clicked behind them. The large room was windowless. Printing machinery was embedded in the concrete floor. A couple of belt-driven presses and a guillotine.

75

Uncut sheets of paper were stacked head-high against the whitewashed wall. A dirty glass partition enclosed a third of the space. Inside were some metal filing cabinets, a table and chairs. Two men were waiting. One was Adam. The other was the stranger she had seen leaving Blake House. He was wearing a shapeless tweed suit and a knitted waistcoat. His ulster was thrown over the back of a chair. He looked at her, scratching the top of his bald head and smiling.

She sat down unsteadily. The air was stuffy, sound without echo. The scar-faced Pole laid his gun on the table. His partner added the spent flashes and empty film packs. He said something in a low voice to Adam. Both left by a concealed door hung with baize.

Adam took her hand. His voice was solicitous. "Do not be alarmed. You were superb."

He touched flame to her cigarette.

She took off her coat, shaking her hair free. "I must talk to you alone," she said in Polish. The stranger's face was ironical.

Adam fingered the strip of beard along his jawline. "You may talk," he assured her.

She shook her head obstinately. "I have always seen you alone. It was understood. Why is this person here?"

He chided her gently. "He is a friend, Wanda. Remember — complete trust and obedience!" It was the first time he had ever called her by her given name. The pungency of peppermint filled her nostrils.

"This man was in Hunter's apartment tonight," she said deliberately. "I met him coming out."

Adam sat down at the table. "In the building, not the apartment."

The other man's Polish was fluent with the accent of the Baltic seaboard.

"Your presence of mind was admirable, Countess. Since we are going to be collaborators, allow me to say that you are not only an extremely attractive woman but a resourceful one."

She looked at him guardedly. He was very certain of himself. His use of her name worried her. Adam's reassurance came quickly, as if he read her mind.

"Stanley is a friend of Hunter's. You can trust him implicitly."

"A friend?" she asked sharply.

Adam's smile was amused. "A friend as you are a friend. You had no trouble with him?"

She crossed her legs nonchalantly. "No. He'd been telephoning my home. He was fairly drunk when I reached the apartment. He talked. You were right, Adam. There's something planned with Korwin. Something that's due to take place on Sunday. And Hunter knows about it. He won't tell me what. It would be dangerous, he said. He wants me to translate a message from Polish into English and help him find someone with a shortwave sender."

The two men exchanged quick glances. "You've no idea where this message is?" said Adam.

"I've an idea," she answered steadily. She took the two coins from her bag and laid them on the table. Benstead moved a little closer to Adam. Both men stared at the sixpenny pieces. Adam opened a steel cabinet. A button in the base of the stand operated a light in the magnifying glass he produced. He adjusted the depth of focus, turning the coins over and over. Benstead gave him a spring-loaded balance.

Adam took a sixpenny bit from his pocket and weighed it. He repeated the maneuver with the coins she had brought, brooding thoughtfully.

Benstead leaned over his shoulder. He took one of the coins and held it under the strong light again, concentrating on the milled edges. His hands worked persistently, locking and twisting. Suddenly the coin split in half, revealing a hollow space. A tiny band of heavier metal had been soldered round the edge, compensating for the silver removed. He did the same with the second coin. Both were empty.

Adam took them in his hands. His voice was very quiet. "Microfilm. Why didn't you mention these coins when you phoned?"

She lifted a hand lazily. "You didn't give me a chance. You told me to go back to the flat immediately and hung up."

Benstead eased an itch in his back against the edge of a filing cabinet.

"Did he say anything about having seen anyone earlier tonight?"

She was aware of their joint scrutiny and cleared her throat defensively.

"He said that he'd been attacked on his way home from the *Quest* offices. Two men stopped his car and searched him. And someone had been in the flat. He made it plain that they missed whatever they were looking for. He mentioned nobody else."

Adam adjusted the carnation in his buttonhole. "We know what it is they were looking for — the film. It could be anywhere. He went to his office. He might well have left it there. If we'd known about the coins earlier . . ."

Benstead's shadow projected across the table. "It's too late to start worrying about that. Hunter's going to wake up in a cell, bewildered and aggressive. Someone's got to restore his confidence. Countess Yampolska is the obvious person."

"You mean I should go to the court?" she asked. The idea disturbed her.

Benstead crunched on one of his pastilles. "You'll *have* to go." He turned to Adam. "I've just had another idea. He needs a shortwave radio rig and someone he can trust. We'll supply them. You'd better stop that pair going back to his apartment. I'll see that the coins are returned."

The Pole gave them to him together with the key to Hunter's flat.

"What'll happen to him?" he asked.

Benstead smoothed the thin hair over his ears. The corners of his mouth turned down.

"He'll be fined. I'll have a lawyer there. Where were these coins, Wanda?"

She looked up, accepting his familiarity. The feeling was growing that he would be a powerful ally.

"In a glass ashtray. You'll see it by his typewriter on the table."

Adam's fingers had been drumming to an unheard melody. He suspended it, looking at Benstead meaningly.

"Then I'll leave everything to you."

Benstead pulled on his ulster. "Exactly. I will be at Bow Street Police Court at ten in the morning. Do you know where that is?"

She moved her head in assent. "Ten o'clock."

He waved and was gone. Adam waited till he heard the door close at the end of the passage. He came to his feet, fitting a cigarette into his holder.

"You're not afraid, are you, Wanda?"

She looked at him, a faint smile holding on her face. "Afraid of what?"

His eyes were remote behind the daik lens. "We cannot afford to fail now. You realize this, don't you? They will accept no excuse in Warsaw — nothing but success."

She picked up her bag and buttoned her coat. "I'm not afraid, Adam," she said truthfully.

He came as far as the door with her, took her hand to his lips.

"Telephone me in the morning. Be careful with Hunter. You left him safely in bed. That is all you know. Good night!"

She ran up the pathway, looking at her watch. It was half-past one. The boisterous wind had swept away the cloud, leaving bright stars nailed to a vaulted sky. Halfway down the slope to St. John's Wood she heard the stutter of a motorcycle engine behind. She slackened speed immediately, thinking of answers to a speed-cop's inquiries. She kept one hand on the wheel, groping with the other for her driving license and car documents. The motorcyclist made no move to overtake. He was no more than a vague muffled shape in the driving mirror. He was still there when she turned into Baker Street. She could see better now. He was a big man, his head hooded in helmet and goggles. He maintained the same precise distance between them all the way back to Fulham.

She parked in front of her house and ran up the steps. The hall was in darkness. Her father was still out. She stood behind the curtains in the sitting room, looking out into the street. After a while, she heard the motorcycle kicked to life. Its staccato roar faded into the distance.

Benjamin du Sautoy-Smith

21 February 1967

HE PAID OFF the cab near the Cenotaph and walked back towards Trafalgar Square. Rain bombarded the somber fa-
çades of the ministry buildings. The usual detail of police
was sheltering at the entrance to Downing Street. He turned
right into a narrow cul-de-sac. A high brick wall blocked the
end. On the left-hand side was a three-story house with
boarded-up windows. A FOR SALE sign, grimed and tattered
with age, stood in the small front yard. The iron gate swung
open on oiled hinges. He unlocked a side door. A covered
passage ran through to the rear of the house. He struck a
match. A flame flickered on a damp-stained ceiling. He unlocked another door at the end of the passage and stepped
into the garden. The windows over his head were boarded-up
as well. The gray roof of a concrete bomb shelter showed at
ground level.

Walls enclosed the garden on both sides and at the bottom.
He picked his way along the muddied path, protecting his
head from the downpour with his umbrella. The door in
the end wall opened into another garden. The flower beds
here were tended. Pieces of statuary glimmered on the
soaked lawn. He ran down some steps and touched a bell.

Two long rings, two short. The man who let him in was in messenger's uniform. He wore a row of military ribbons and mirrorlike boots. He snapped to attention before shutting the door behind Smith.

"The D.D.'s upstairs in his room, sir."

A flight of stairs led from lower to upper hall. Candle-lamps were set in the pine-paneled walls. There was a William-and-Mary clock, a couple of Turner landscapes. The polished parquet floor smelled of beeswax. The only sound was the ticking of the clock. A gold-banded umbrella dripped in a stand. He put his own beside it. He ran upstairs, combing his sandy hair with his fingers. He rapped on the door in front of him.

Books covered the walls. An unlit chandelier hung from the high ceiling, reflecting the blaze of the coal fire. A short man was standing in front of the fireplace. He unhooked his heels from the brass fender, holding his hand out in welcome. Everything about him was neat — herringbone tweeds, immaculate brown brogues, the thatch of gray hair. His dominant feature was his washed-blue eyes. They held Smith in a steady inspection. His smile showed a pipe-smoker's mouth, the teeth in the lower jaw chipped and stained. He kicked one of the two leather chairs in Smith's direction. Smith waited till the older man was seated. A sudden flurry of rain lashed the curtained windows. Smith stretched his damp trouser-legs nearer the fire. He stayed silent, knowing that the General would set his own pace. Quick, strong fingers crammed tobacco into the bowl of meerschaum. The sucking was loud till a blue cloud obscured the other's face.

"Now, Benjy."

Smith sank a little further down on his shoulder blades.

"I suppose an apology's in order, sir. I couldn't get hold of you earlier."

The General fished an old-fashioned silver watch from his pocket and looked at it.

"I can give you an hour, Benjy. What's up?"

Smith stared past his toes into the fire. "I can't be sure yet, sir. You remember Benstead?"

The General laid his watch on the desk in front of him. His head tilted back, his eyes consulting the ceiling.

"That's the chess player, isn't it — one of your bird dogs. I remember his file, yes. Well?"

"He telephoned me this evening with what sounded like a very odd story. If it turns out the way I think it might, we could be on to something important, sir."

The General's pipe was under control. "Let's skip the 'sir' for the rest of the evening. What was the story?"

Smith told it. The Deputy Director listened, eyes half closed, sucking noisily on his pipe. He rose and knocked the bowl out on the edge of the mantel. A series of charred rings was already there. He swung round, pointing his pipe at Smith.

"Assault and Burglary — and nothing to show for it! I can see the Director's face when he hears about this. And you believe Hunter's story, obviously."

Smith wriggled his shoulders. "With qualifications, yes."

"Qualifications." The General shook his head. "I should have known it. What do we have on Hunter?"

Smith's trouser-legs were steaming. He shifted them away from the fire.

"Not too much, I'm afraid, sir. I've told Reconnaissance to get a fix on him. But he *does* work for *Quest* — he *has* been to Poland and the stuff he writes touts right-wing thinking. Benstead says he's a boozer. I know that he's belligerent."

"So you decided that the firm couldn't use him." The General's smile was frosty.

Smith made no secret of his impressions of the Canadian. "I wouldn't use him except in the last resort, sir. My feeling is that as much as anything he wants a story for his magazine. He's one of these crusaders. The girl and the boy alone are enough. This thing is made to order for him."

The General hooked his heels over the brass fender, giving himself more height.

"If he tries that we'll get a D-notice slapped on him. I'll tell you what *I* feel, Benjy. That we ought to pass the whole thing through channels and forget it. Political asylum means going to the Home Office again. They haven't been very helpful recently. The Director doesn't like getting his knuckles rapped. A pick-up like this would take a great deal of organization and time's short. And what would the firm be getting in return — nothing! I see economic sabotage of this kind as having propaganda value. And as such it doesn't concern us. Why not simply wrap up the job and pass it to someone else?"

Smith looked up, his voice quietly telling. "Suppose we were getting something more than just economic sabotage. Suppose we were getting Kyril Malek?"

The Deputy Director's hand stopped halfway to his ear. "Did you say *Malek,* Benjy?" he asked incredulously. "He's still in a fortress in the Tatras with fifteen years to serve. Either that or dead." A green telephone buzzed on the desk. He touched a button and silenced it. Pale blue eyes searched Smith's face.

"Suppose he'd escaped," Smith said after a while. "The *Bezpieka* wouldn't be exactly anxious to advertise it."

The General pushed a hammered silver box across the desk and refilled his pipe.

"Malek," he repeated thoughtfully. "You've sent a signal to the Embassy of course?"

Smith chose a Perfecto and lit it. "The reply came an hour ago. They don't know anything. None of our people in Warsaw know anything. This is a feeling I have, sir. Malek was a lone wolf. He would organize but he wouldn't be organized. We know of him. He doesn't know of us. He wouldn't go to any of the obvious contacts, assuming he knew them. He's been in jail for five years, remember. Hunter is just the sort of chap he would pick on."

The General took a turn past the bookshelves, ten paces, swing round then back again. He stopped in front of the fire.

"*Convince* me that Korwin is Malek, Benjy."

Smith dribbled smoke from his nose. "At the moment I can't, sir. I told you — this is a hunch on my part. But there are points of similarity. Korwin is in his mid-forties — so would Malek be. Malek lisped. So does Korwin. The steel teeth could have been added at any time. Malek is a hard loser. It would be typical of him to come back to us leaving half a dozen exploded power stations behind. My bet is that we'll find a safety signal in Hunter's message — something that proves Malek is Korwin."

The General's voice was testy. "We're back to the bloody message. What am I supposed to say to the Director — 'Malek is back. He's going to be in Potsdam on Sunday waiting for a pick-up. We don't know where and we don't know when. Because the officer in charge of Planning refused to accept the signal'?"

Smith answered doggedly. "If you do that, sir, you'll have to tell him why. Tell him that I believe Hunter to be a dangerous and unreliable contact."

The General sat behind the desk again. "Then just what do you propose, Benjy?"

Smith lifted his head. "Give me twenty-four hours, sir. I'll make myself responsible for them. If I fail, then we'll go to Hunter and the Director will have to think up a way of silencing him afterwards."

The General put his watch back on its chain. He hefted it, looking across the desk warningly.

"All right, Benjy. Twenty-four hours. After that we'll have Hunter in. For God's sake keep your nose clean. If you draw men from the College, I don't want to hear about it."

Smith straightened his jacket, hiding his grin. The spare man watching him was concerned with one thing only — results. Nevertheless he had a fierce and waspy dislike of bureaucratic criticism. Criticism that the firm's unorthodox method of enforcement sometimes provoked.

"I'll keep my nose clean," he promised. "Good night, sir."

He went out through the front door. The short street ran parallel to the cul-de-sac behind — a dark tunnel with rain bouncing from the roofs. The Georgian houses had long ceased to be homes. Most were used as offices. The door he had just left bore a sign reading

MINISTRY OF DEFENCE *(Department of Reeducation and Orientation)*
NO CALLERS EXCEPT BY APPOINTMENT

A television camera concealed in the wall completed the warning. Deserted by night, the street maintained a daytime anonymity enjoyed by those who worked there. Callers at number seventeen were infrequent. Spreading elms and high brick walls screened the arrival of those who came by the same way as Smith had used.

A pool car was waiting, the driver a girl in green uniform with sergeant's chevrons. He recognized her face as someone who had driven him before. He settled back, relieved to be spared the chore of having to give directions. He needed to concentrate on Hunter. The D.D. had given him twenty-four hours. He might be able to stretch it to forty-eight. Despite his boast in the library he had no definite plan for dealing with the Canadian. At the back of his mind he was irritated that for the first time in years he was letting personal dislike color his judgment.

It was becoming an obsession with him to deal with Hunter in *his* way. The man stood for everything he disliked. He searched his brain for a lead. More force was impractical, which left guile. The fix he'd asked for on Hunter would be complete by the morning — or as complete as the time allowed. He'd know then how Hunter lived and thought. The knowledge would give him the clue what to do.

He stopped the driver at the foot of Kew Bridge. The lively wind had swept away the rain. A glitter of stars had been left overhead. Summer and winter, he walked the last quarter of a mile to his house at night. He passed the Royal Botanical Gardens and kept going till he reached a lane. He turned down it, seeing the outline of the house fronting the river. It perched on piles, swathed in weed, jutting into the swirling current. The owner of the neighboring boatyard had built and grown tired of it. Smith had lived there eleven years. His nearest neighbor was two hundred yards away. The lane stopped at the gates to a boatyard. A passage led between the ribbed hulls of unfinished craft. Oak planks stacked for seasoning sharpened the washed air with a smell that was faintly vinegar. The passage ended abruptly on a muddy towpath. The twenty-odd feet to the house was bridged by a plank gangway. The exterior of the one-story structure was finished in pebble-dash. Black-painted lathes made diagonal patterns on the walls. The weather vane was in the shape of a rooster. It swung now noisily.

The loneliness of the house comforted him. He was no longer aware of its ugliness. He walked up the gangway. The back of the entrance door was hung with bookshelves. With the door closed, the large sitting room had the aspect of a ship's saloon. Porthole-styled windows overlooked water that was ten feet deep even at low tide. A pair of irascible swans made their home in the dark green shadows beneath the house.

The architecture was boxlike. Bedroom, sitting room, bathroom and kitchen. The fumed-oak furniture, faded carpets and Benares brass were relics of the Suffolk rectory where he had grown up. Other than the Chinese prints of prancing white horses and his clothes, little of what was there had been chosen by him.

He put his briefcase on the Formica-topped table that served as a desk. There were two telephones. One green, one black. There was a calendar, a picture of his mother, serene-faced with fair hair piled high on her head. Apart from these the table was empty. He stood his umbrella in the kitchen sink and filled a jug at the faucet. A couple of pots of azaleas stood on a ledge where they caught most light. He watered each plant carefully. An ex-Marine sergeant came three times a week, collecting the contents of the trash baskets for Security disposal. He cleaned house for an hour, running the hoover like an assault weapon. Each time he squared Smith's bed-making so that sheets and blankets presented barrack-room conformity.

Smith's sister, on her rare visits, complained that the house lacked charm — that it needed a woman's touch. The criticism left him unmoved. He thought of women as he did all forms of art — occasionally decorative, too frequently futile. There was no chimneyplace. He switched on a heater and opened a window. The dinghy below bumped against the old tire wrapped round a pier. A ladder was fastened against the outside wall. Sometimes he left the house this way, sculling across the river and leaving the dinghy moored to the opposite bank. He rowed in gloves and wearing a bowler hat, deaf to the ribaldry of passing tug-masters. The maneuver had the same value for him as a dozen others. His telephone listing: Benjamin du Sautoy-Smith M.A. His place on the committee of the All-England Tennis Club. His conscientious attendance at sessions of the Services Judo Circle. Each image was valid and created to weaken its fellows.

He brewed himself a cup of cocoa and carried it to the table. Rubber bands circled the brown folder he had brought with him. He removed them. Two photographs stared back at him. The first was passport-size, showing a face like a tom-cat's — wide through the cheekbones and narrowing to a pointed chin. Tufts of black hair sprouted over the ears, heightening the feline illusion. The second picture was full-length, taken against a white backdrop calibrated in feet and inches. The same face was recognizable in spite of the cropped head and spectacles. The subject was dressed in workman's overalls. He was looking directly into the lens of the camera, smiling slightly as if the photographer had just said something funny.

Smith turned the page. The newspaper clipping was dated 20th August 1961.

BRITON ARRESTED IN CRACOW HOTEL

Cracow. August 18.—An affray in the corridors of the Hotel Europejski ended with the arrest of a man giving his name as Bernard Lecky, 42, a free-lance photographer of Shoot-Up Hill, London N.W. Mr. Lecky, a visitor to Poland, was accosted by two men outside his hotel bedroom late yesterday evening. An American, witness of the ensuing scene, stated that the men tried to seize Mr. Lecky who resisted vigorously. Blows were struck during the scuffle. Mr. Lecky was seen to leave the hotel in the company of the two men. Members of the Security Militia arrived later and removed Mr. Lecky's effects from his room. A spokesman for the Foreign Ministry here stated that charges of spying and sabotage would be brought against Mr. Lecky. Until such time as the charges were formulated he would be held *incommunicado*.

Smith flicked another page. The decoded message was brief and dated 14th September 1962.

TOP SECRET   URGENT   WRSW

Mlk sentenced twenty years military-court today stop removed unknown destination under company-strength armed guard stop equipment seized included thirty pounds W.D. issue strip plastic explosive stop

He replaced the photographs and closed the folder on the rest of the typewritten sheets. He sat for a while, sipping his cocoa. A train rattled along a distant viaduct, the lighted coaches showing high above the rooftops. Water slapped against the boatyard pier. Instinct and experience assured him that Malek was Korwin. And the firm needed Malek. He took his cup into the kitchen, washed it and set his breakfast tray. The meal never varied. A wilted half-section of grapefruit, two slices of wholemeal bread-and-butter. He dropped a tea bag into a tarnished silver pot. A rowing machine was bolted to the floor outside the bathroom. He stripped to his shorts and lowered himself on the seat. He sculled the air methodically. In-OUT. In-OUT. His breath whined through his nostrils noisily. After ten minutes of it, he showered the sweat from his body and went into the spartan bedroom. The clothes closet was open. A uniform bearing the insignia of a lieutenant-colonel hung at the end of the row of suits. There was a small collection of books in a case by the bed. An anthology of John Buchan, some paperbacks, a three-volume copy of Pepys' *Diary*, Small's *History of Suffolk Families*.

The dresser was as unadorned as his desk. A pair of hairbrushes backed with yellowed ivory, a nail file like a rasp, a second picture of his mother. He had slept in the bed for thirty years. The mattress was contoured and indented by his bony shape. A sampler-framed text dangled from a hook over the bedhead, spotted with fly-specks. PUT NOT THY TRUST IN MAN.

The affirmation was as near to a complete philosophy as he could imagine. He switched off the lights and composed himself for sleep.

Hamish Hunter

22 February 1967

He turned over, groaning. His body was aching in half a dozen places. Gummed eyes opened on small squares of glass set in a metal frame high in the wall. The bed he was lying on was made of solid wood sunk in cement. He lifted himself on an elbow. The thin stinking blanket dropped on the concrete floor. A bare lavatory bowl stood in the left-hand corner of the cell. No chain. A metal slide flushed the cistern concealed behind the glazed brick wall. The steel door was painted battleship gray. A message had been scratched on it. *Go back before it's too late.*

High in the ceiling, a yellow bulb burned behind thick protective glass. He swung his feet to the ground, feeling automatically for a cigarette. There were none in his pocket. All he could find was some money, his keys and a couple of letters addressed to him at the office. He opened his fingers slowly, staring at the dried mud on his trousers and trying to remember. There was more mud on his shoes. He bent down, inspecting them. He'd put on his own shoes. They were tied with the double-knots he always used.

His mind groped back to a dim impression of a room — a light somewhere near the floor — a bell ringing. A *telephone* bell, that was it. Memory assembled the pieces painfully till the puzzle was almost complete. Only the key pieces evaded him. He had been lying in his bed. The light near the floor was the glow from the electric heater. Then somehow Wanda had been there. He must have gotten up. He recalled her helping him back to bed. He'd called her at home but that had been earlier. *To tell her about the film.* She'd given him seltzer and left.

He moved his furred tongue cautiously. He must have gone to sleep and awakened again. Then presumably he'd dressed and gone out. What came next was anyone's guess. The fact was that for the second time in his life he'd waked up in a police cell. This time with no idea how he came to be there. It was nice going.

There was a plastic cup on the table. He filled it under the spigot and drained the water at a gulp. When his brain no longer functioned properly, it was time to take the pledge. His watch was still on his wrist. A quarter to nine. The thought gave him a jolt. The sooner he was out of this place the better. People were waiting for him at the office. He went over to the door and beat on it with the heels of his hands. Footsteps rang along the corridor. A hatch in the door was lowered. The cop's head was framed in the outside light. He was young and his curly hair glistened with pomade.

His smile was good-humored. "How'd you feel now, mate?"

Hunter rubbed his scalp. "Terrible."

The hatch closed and the cell door opened. The cop stood back, sniffing dramatically.

"Out you come. What were you drinking, nitroglycerine?"

Hunter stepped forward gingerly. There were more glazed bricks. A steel door blocked the end of the corridor. He steadied himself as the cop unlocked it. They climbed a flight of stairs to the lobby. A sweet smell of rotting fruit filtered through swing doors leading to the street. Hunter recognized the dingy façade opposite. He was in Bow Street Police Station. The cop jerked his head. The board on the door said CHARGE ROOM.

"In you go, mate. And smile."

The barred windows were dirty. A waist-high counter split the room in two. Behind it were a couple of desks. WANTED posters hung beneath an institutional clock. A sergeant was sitting at one of the desks, reading a newspaper. He lowered it slowly and turned his head. His hair was brick-red, his round face freckled. The jacket of his uniform bulged in all the wrong places. Hunter's escort waved a hand.

"The Sleeping Beauty, sarge."

The sergeant rose lethargically. He came across on flat feet, took a short look at Hunter and grunted.

"What court's he down for — number two? See he gets a razor on those whiskers. All right, dasher, let's have your name." He opened a ledger on the counter and flicked a pen at the floor.

Hunter eyed him hostilely. He'd been searched. They must have seen the letters in his pocket.

"You know it already," he said wearily.

The sergeant was less affable than his colleague. He leaned his weight on his forearms.

"Listen, mister, we like *you* to supply the information. You weren't exactly what I'd call talkative last time I saw you."

The young cop was standing on the sergeant's blind side.

94

He lowered an eyelid meaningly. Hunter received the message.

"Hamish Hunter. Forty years old. Journalist. Address, number two, Blake House, Chelsea Embankment. That's South-West Three. What's the charge?"

The sergeant's flamboyant backhand was occupying all his attention. He added a final flourish before looking up.

"You've got two. 'Drunk and Incapable' and 'Committing a Public Nuisance.' "

Hunter blinked. " 'Committing a Public Nuisance.' What's that supposed to mean?"

The sergeant dropped the cover of the charge-book. Red fuzz grew between the knuckles of his fingers.

"It's just that it sounds better than 'pissing on tombstones.' "

Hunter swallowed with difficulty. His hands and legs were unsteady. A dull thudding punctuated the ache in his temples. He saw the piece hot off the presses of the afternoon newspapers. JOURNALIST ARRESTED ON INDECENCY CHARGES.

"Can I use the phone?" he said suddenly.

The sergeant shook his head. "You don't need no phone. You got all the answers, haven't you — how many times you been in before?"

The knowing look triggered Hunter's anger. "You've got my name and address and that's all you're going to get. You don't like it, take it up with my lawyer."

The sergeant's face mottled. He spread his legs dangerously. "One of those, are you? Well let me tell you, *Mister* Hunter. I don't care if you're God's cousin. You're in the nick. Get him out of here," he said to the younger officer.

There was a recess at the end of the corridor downstairs.

A square of mirror was stuck on the wall above the washbasin. Hunter did his best with blunt blade, cold water and yellow soap. He scraped his face clean painfully — scrubbed his teeth with the corner of his handkerchief. His escort lounged against the wall behind, watching curiously. He fished a couple of cigarettes from a pack and gave them to Hunter. He pointed up at the ceiling.

"Failed C.I.D. He's just frustrated. He's not as bad as he sounds. You made a pig of yourself," he went on conversationally. "You realize they had to carry you in here?"

Hunter wiped the blade. The next user would have fun. "I was tired," he said simply.

The cop held out a match. "There was someone here to see you half an hour ago. An elderly bloke with a bald head. Said he was a friend of yours. You were still sleeping."

Hunter's quick look made his head dizzy. "How did he know I was here?"

The cop shrugged. "Search me. He said he'd be back with your lawyer. Told me to tell you he'd get in touch with your office. Work for some newsmagazine, don't you?"

Hunter dragged deep on his butt. Nothing made sense. For all he knew, he might have *been* with Benstead. It was like groping for a ghost in a fog.

"There wasn't anyone else here — a woman?" The cop shook his head. Hunter felt his face tentatively. The skin was red-raw. "Any chance of some tea?"

It arrived with a square of chalk-white bread spread with margarine. He cradled the enameled mug with his hands and sipped the brew gratefully. The blackout was something he had to accept. How much he let other people know of his acceptance was a tricky point. It was no time for Toronto to start thinking that they had an alcoholic on their hands. He could bet blind on everyone at the London bureau. Marty would block any report likely to filter back to Canada. Wanda was the problem. Right now he needed her the worst way. She'd have to understand how seriously he took this whole thing. He smiled, fancying himself at an Alcoholics Anonymous meeting — the gospel-hungry faces turned as he rose to his feet. He was still smiling when the door opened. The young cop had his cap on.

"Pick up your monkeys and parrots — don't leave nothing behind. You won't be coming back — I hope."

The lobby outside the magistrates' courts was crowded. A sad thin blonde in a stained camel's hair coat stood next to a policewoman. The scarecrow behind them wore a straggle of matted beard and a mac belted with cord. A JESUS SAVES sign was on the floor near his feet. Hard-eyed plainclothesmen chatted to their prisoners. Their roving glances held Hunter for a second and then dismissed him. A cop detached himself from a group of uniformed police and strolled over. He nodded at Hunter's escort.

"OK, Harry! And how do *you* feel this morning?"

Hunter eyed him without pleasure. The man was a complete stranger.

"How about yourself?"

The cop looked pained. *"Me?* I'm on night-duty, mate. If it wasn't for you I'd have been in kip three hours ago. There's some people here to see you."

They were standing near the probation officer's room. Benstead, Wanda and a man dressed in striped trousers and a black jacket. The cop drifted away a few feet. Wanda wore a blue reefer coat. Her dark hair was bound in an Alice-

97

band. Weals showed under her eyes as if she had been weeping. He took her in his arms with sudden fierce tenderness.

"I'm sorry." His mouth was buried in her hair. The whisper was the best he could do.

She lifted her head. "Don't worry, darling," she said steadily. "I'm with you all the way." There was no criticism in her voice — only the promise of help. His fingers thanked and let her go.

Benstead's hat had dried to a new rakish shape. "You're full of surprises, Hamish." He offered his long-toothed grin. "This is Mr. Wells, your solicitor."

Hunter nodded briefly. The man had a thin mouth and mournful manner.

"It isn't a funeral. I mean, good God, I didn't kill anyone. I just got drunk." The remark was intended for them all.

Benstead looked as if sleep had evaded him. "A couple of kids from the agencies are in the press box. I know them both. There won't be any write-up. Nevertheless, you'd better listen to what Mr. Wells has to say."

The lawyer made fluttering movements with his fingers. "I'd be a lot happier if we were facing a simple charge of 'Drunk and Incapable,' Mr. Hunter. The second charge is unfortunate. We're up in front of a magistrate who's hot on this type of offense. I understand there's a previous conviction, isn't there?"

Hunter felt himself redden. The man made him sound like a criminal. He was conscious of Wanda's eyes. They never left his face for a second.

"I was fined a few months ago. Obstructing a police officer in the execution of his duty. That's what they called it."

Wells scribbled with a gold pencil. "I've had a word with

the arresting officer. There's nothing doing there, I'm afraid. I'd say our only course is to plead guilty."

Hunter put the question frankly. "Suppose I told the truth — that I just don't remember?"

"No defense at all," Wells said primly. "This is a court, not a clinic."

"So what do they do — send me to jail?"

The lawyer's smile carried the weight of professional reassurance.

"No — it won't come to that. Just let me handle things. Above all don't antagonize the magistrate."

They turned, hearing Hunter's name called from the courtroom door. He climbed a couple of steps into a dock facing the magistrate's bench. He looked round uncertainly. The witness stand was on his left, the press box on his right. Wells had taken a seat near the two men already sitting there. Wanda and Benstead were in the front row of the public benches. She was still watching him, indifferent to the seedy courtroom customers surrounding her. There had been no time to ask how she and Benstead had met. Enough to know that she was not there alone. The jailer touched his shoulder. He sat down facing the magistrate.

A clerk rose, reading from the paper in front of him. "This is number two on the sheet, Your Worship. Hamish Hunter, you are charged in that about twelve-forty-five A.M. on this day you were drunk and incapable outside St. Luke's Church, Adelphi Terrace, in the City of Westminster. Do you plead guilty or not guilty?"

Wells came to his feet easily, fingers hooked in his waistcoat pocket.

"I appear for the defendant. He pleads guilty."

The clerk continued. "You are further charged in that at the same time and place you committed a public nuisance. Do you plead guilty or not guilty?"

"Guilty," said Wells. He resumed his seat and glanced over at Hunter, tapping his teeth with the gold pencil.

The court stenographer's lips moved soundlessly, close to his recording machine. The magistrate had the head of a Dickensian banker. A thin doubting nose and a mouth that looked permanently depressed. He wore a wing collar with a black stock and pearl pin. His deliberate voice heightened the impression of dated manners.

"Very well. We might as well have the facts."

The arresting constable took the stand. He rattled through the oath-taking and drew a deep breath.

"Police-constable Jepson, sir, C. Division. At approximately twelve-forty A.M. today I was on duty with other officers in a patrol van. As a result of a message received, we proceeded to St. Luke's Church, Adelphi Terrace. There I found the defendant stretched out on the steps leading to the porch. I asked him what he was doing there. He was incapable of making any reply or getting up. I formed the impression that he was intoxicated and took him into custody, sir. He was subsequently charged. There's no medical evidence in this case."

The magistrate leaned his chin on his hand and stared down at Hunter.

"What about the second charge, officer. What do you say about that?"

The constable glanced at his notes. "I understand that the lady who made the emergency call complained that the defendant had been staggering about in the churchyard, urinating, sir."

Wells was quickly on his feet. "It's my duty to ask if this person is being called to give evidence — otherwise this is hearsay. The officer's saying that he didn't receive the call himself."

The magistrate turned towards the witness box. "Is the witness in court?"

The constable hesitated. "No, sir."

The magistrate shrugged. "I don't see that it makes any difference, Mr. Wells. You've pleaded guilty. No matter. Tell us what you *saw*, constable."

Jepson ducked his head. "When I found the defendant, sir, his trousers were in a state of disarray."

Someone at the back of the court sniggered. The magistrate's sharp eye found the offender and silenced him.

"Very well, thank you, constable. I suppose you'll want to say something, Mr. Wells?" His tone discouraged the idea.

Wells came to his feet again. He began confidently enough. "Your Worship, I make no suggestion that the officer is not telling the entire truth. My instructions are that the defendant has been working under intense pressure for some time. He is a journalist of international repute. Only yesterday he returned from an assignment that had taken him behind the Iron Curtain for three weeks. He is *not* a man who drinks habitually. There is strong reason to believe that the cause of this — this *lapse* stems from extreme mental stress. He asks me to convey his sincere apologies to the court. I am hoping that in this case Your Worship may see fit to adopt a certain course . . ." he paused expectantly.

The magistrate adjusted rimless spectacles. "Is anything known about this man?"

The jailer stood, drawing in his stomach. He read from a typewritten sheet.

"On 14th October, 1966, he was fined £15 at West London Police Court for 'Drunk and Disorderly' and 'Obstructing a Police Officer.' There's nothing else, Your Worship."

The magistrate brooded for a couple of seconds. "I hope you're not thinking in terms of an Absolute Discharge, Mr. Wells. He pleaded guilty and there's nothing in what you say that justifies his disgraceful behavior."

Wells came in smoothly. "With all due respect, sir, there's the matter of his professional reputation. His friends tell me that Hunter is literally on the verge of a mental breakdown. I was only instructed at nine o'clock this morning. There has been no time to bring medical evidence. But with Your Worship's approval, arrangements have been made for him to see a Harley Street specialist."

The jailer's swift move came too late to prevent Hunter from springing up and grabbing the dock rail.

"I've pleaded guilty," he said in a loud clear voice. "I don't *need* a doctor."

He found himself being tugged down from behind. The jailer's heavy hand pinned him in his seat. He heard Benstead's urgent whisper and looked across at the press bench. One of the men there shook his head warningly. Hunter's nails dug into his palms.

The magistrate's voice was unruffled. "It's possible that you're right, judging from that outburst, Mr. Wells. When is his appointment?"

"Three o'clock this afternoon," Wells said. "It was the best we could do."

The magistrate's head moved slowly up and down. "Very well. Hunter! I'm remanding you twenty-four hours for sentence in your own surety of fifty pounds. Next case!"

Hunter walked down the steps. The constable ushered him into an office where he signed bail papers. They went back to the lobby. Wells was in a corner, talking to Wanda and Benstead. He cleared his throat as he saw Hunter coming.

"All over bar the shouting," he said. "He *likes* medical evidence, Mr. Hunter. He'll fine you, of course. I'd say a tenner, no more." The bland face was set in self-congratulation.

"Thanks," Hunter said shortly.

Wells looked at the clock. "I must away — I'm due at the Guildhall. I'll see you tomorrow. Don't forget three o'clock. Mr. Benstead has the address." He smiled, half-bowed to Wanda and hurried down the steps.

Hunter watched him go. "Clown," he said finally. He took Wanda's elbow. "What I need is a strong cup of coffee. Come on, Stanley."

Outside a brisk wind was blowing from the northeast. Pigeons soared on it, skimming the television masts that bristled on the rooftops. Hunter shortened his stride to match Wanda's. Everything was colorful after the drabness of the cells. He breathed properly for the first time in hours. They started walking towards the Strand. They had gone fifty yards when Hunter stopped suddenly. He pushed Wanda through a door between steamed windows. Benstead went on a few feet before he realized that he was alone. He turned hurriedly and followed. He came into the café looking at Hunter questioningly. Hunter ignored him. He was watching the street. The man reading a newspaper passed the door without a sidelong glance. He'd been in court, sitting directly behind Wanda. It just could be coincidence — an even chance. The guy had to turn left or right on leaving the building.

Hunter led the way to a table at the back of the eating-place. He was getting jumpy. They sat under a mirror chalked with particulars of the day's fare. A tired waitress took their order. She jerked three espressos and brought them to the table. Hunter drank his straight.

"Maybe you won't believe this," he said carefully. "But what I said was true — I don't remember a thing after going to bed last night."

Benstead chased the sugar round his cup with a spoon. He looked up, eyes serious.

"*I* believe it. I happened to be on the street at half-past eight this morning. Murphy'd had the tip from one of the police drivers. The description was the same — the name. They found letters in your pocket. It seemed to me that someone had better do something. I got Wells."

"I won't forget it, Stanley. How'd you get hold of Wanda?" Hunter asked curiously.

Benstead pushed at a lank wisp of hair. "I phoned your office. Borgerund said he thought she ought to know. He gave me her number."

Hunter reached out and cupped Wanda's hands in his own. "And what about Borgerund?"

Benstead lifted his shoulders. "Don't worry — everyone's

on your side. Look, I'll leave you two alone. Don't forget the doctor, Hamish. It's a routine thing. Pressure of work — maybe you took a sleeping pill after drink. I don't know. Anyway, here's the address." He pushed over a slip of paper.

He stood up, shrugging into the shabby ulster. "Telephone me tonight. Any time after nine. If there's anything you want doing, let me know. And take care of her, Hamish. She's worth it." He covered his head with his hat, lifted it at Wanda and was gone.

Hunter tugged her wrists gently. "Was I drunk when you left me, darling? Be honest."

Her face clouded. "I should have stayed, then none of this would have happened. I blame myself more than you. But it's over now — isn't it, Hamish?"

He nodded, leaning across the table. "I'm on the wagon, if that's what you mean. You know what I told you happened to me yesterday — the mugging — the flat being searched? Did you believe it?"

Dark blue eyes met his candidly. "Of course I believe it."

His voice was low and insistent. "And you know what they were after. Seven hours of my life are missing since then. Do you think there could be a connection?"

Lines gathered between the black sable of her eyebrows. "I've done nothing but think about this ever since you told me. I love you. When you're in danger, I'm in danger. Just the same, I'm a woman — how *can* I know about these things? But I know what makes sense. You were drunk when I left you last night. Whatever happened afterwards was your own doing. I'm sure of it."

He finished the last of his coffee. What she said only confirmed his own feeling.

"Have you got time — what about the club?"

She checked her watch. "Half-past eleven. I told them I had to go to the dentist, this morning and all day tomorrow." Something in her eyes made him ask. "All day *tomorrow*." She opened her handbag and gave him a clipping. His pulse quickened as he read it. The half-page was torn from a Polish émigré journal.

OPENING OF NEW FACTORY MARKS PILSUDSKI DAY

One of England's most up-to-date electronic factories went into full-scale production yesterday. The plant, occupying seven acres in Rainham, Essex, is the brain-child of Doctor Jerzy Kowarski, eminent Polish scientist. Dr. Kowarski first came to England in 1943 and was engaged in top-secret work for the British government. Many of his inventions were used in the development of long-distance warning systems. After the cessation of hostilities, Dr. Kowarski entered private enterprise, producing, among other devices, sounding-units for deep-sea fishing, the "Third Eye" system of traffic-control used throughout the U.K. and Australia.

Dr. Kowarski's devotion to the cause of Free Poland, his generous support of émigré charities, need no publicity in these columns. Our illustration shows a reception given by Dr. Kowarski at his Mayfair home. Among those present were Prince and Princess Lublyana, Professor Rudski, General-Count Yampolski and other members of the Polish community in London. The Editor and staff of *Free Poland* extend their heartfelt congratulations to their illustrious countryman.

LONG LIVE POLAND! LONG LIVE KOWARSKI!

A slight man with a spade beard stood in the foreground of the photograph flanked by a number of people drinking champagne. All wore the slightly stunned look fitting the occasion. Wanda's father was directly behind Kowarski.

She watched him anxiously. "I've known him since I was small. He's a good man and loves his country. I had to tell him, darling."

"Tell him *what?*" he asked. Thought of the film, Smith and Korwin, obliterated the memory of the past few hours.

Assurance replaced her anxiety. "That men's lives are in danger. Men who are fighting for a free Poland. He's going to help."

He turned round sharply. There was no one nearer than ten yards away. A boy sucking tea through his teeth.

"How will he help?"

"By sending the message," she said simply. "You don't even have to use your photographer unless you want to. He has dark rooms, every sort of radio equipment possible in the research labs. He'll do it all himself. He asks only one thing."

Hunter's pulse was racing now. "What's that?"

"That his name isn't mentioned. He has a business and family here but he's still an alien. He'll trust me and because of me you. Nobody else. It'll have to be done at night — when the workers are gone."

He felt as though he'd just come out of an oxygen mask. The nausea and trembling had vanished. His head was completely clear.

"Then tomorrow night. You make the arrangements. Will you come as far as the office with me? I need moral support." He smiled.

She gathered her gloves and handbag. "I'll come with you *anywhere.*" He paid his bill at the counter and followed her outside.

They left her car parked and walked west to the *Quest* building. Lights burned on the top floor. He entered the office with a sense of coming home. Typewriters clattered at the end of the passage. A radio was playing in the Research Room. The Coke vending machine was still out of order. The girl at the switchboard looked up as he passed. He tapped hello on the glass partition. Borgerund's blond head came round the door. He opened it wide.

"Hi, Hamish — Wanda! Could I see you a minute, alone, Hamish?"

Standing as he was, he partially blocked sight of the General Office. Camera cases on a chair there told Hunter that Gerry was in the building.

"Sure," he said easily. "Wanda, you go on in and talk to Ginny. I'll be with you in a couple of minutes."

The outside wall was mostly window, the room the same size as his own. It had the same furniture. The flat-topped desk with its back to the light, three good chairs and a closet. Borgerund's secretary had a stall in the General Office. The blond man fished a half-smoked cigar from the ashtray as he walked in.

His voice was hesitant. "We've worked together for five years. If it hadn't been for you I wouldn't have *had* the job." His cigar was dead. He tried to relight it. In the end he mashed it into fragments.

Hunter was in his favorite office position, the edge of the desk supporting his buttocks. He looked at the other man curiously, then grinned.

"I get it," he said lightly. "Uncle Marty's going into the pulpit. He doesn't *like* having to say this but Hamish was naughty." He clapped the palms of his hands together softly.

108

Borgerund lowered himself behind the desk, his expression uncomfortable. He jerked a drawer open and shoved a slip of paper so that it was touching Hunter's knee. Hunter read it without shifting his position.

TORONTO 06 HRS 15

ADVISE HUNTER HIS IMMEDIATE SUSPENSION X BORGERUND APPNTD
ACTING CHIEF OF BUREAU X KILL POLAND COPY AND SOMEONE
OVER THERE STRT THINKING RPT THINKING X FLYING LONDON
SOONEST X DUNN MANGING EDITR XXXXX

He raised his head slowly, staring through the window over the grimy roof of Canada House. Girls on an early lunch-break were feeding the pigeons on the square. Buses bulled their way in and out of the traffic. There were no flags at half-mast, no rataplanplan of drums. He slid from the desk, the nerve jumping under the skin near his eye.

"Congratulations."

Borgerund's hand slammed down on top of the desk. "Goddammit, Hamish, don't make it any tougher for me! How do you think I'm feeling. Nobody — but *nobody* — in the building wants anything but you here where you belong. There isn't a single one who'd rat on you. Wherever Dunn got his dirty little bit of news, it wasn't out of *this* office."

The Telex message was timed six-fifteen. They must have pulled Dunn out of his bed to send it. It was strange. He'd almost forgotten the reason for going to Warsaw. His own story had become dwarfed by a more dramatic one. Suddenly it assumed importance again. Maybe Dunn wouldn't print what he'd written but he'd make sure somebody else did. He did his best with a grin.

"That Dunn — what a comedian. 'Kill Poland copy and start thinking.' Know what, Marty, I think I'm going to spit in his eye when he shows up."

There was sweat on Borgerund's forehead. He took off his jacket and loosened his tie.

"You've got a contract. He can't walk out of it without giving you severance pay."

Hunter nodded wearily. His contract had almost two years to run. If he was fired the Golden Boot would be worth the best part of $40,000.

"Does Ginny know?" he asked suddenly.

Borgerund's broad shoulders rose and fell. "What else, with that camel outside on the Telex machine! Everybody knows. I'm sorry, Hamish. What happened this morning, I mean in court? I gave Benstead Wanda's number. Maybe I was wrong. I just thought. I'd have been there myself but there didn't seem much point."

Hunter dragged his eyes away from the window. "She saved my life — you weren't wrong. I'm up again tomorrow, for sentence. A tenner fine and some moralizing from the bench. That's the way it goes. OK, Marty. Let me know as soon as Dunn flies in. I'll keep in touch. And keep thinking, hear now?"

The passage was a gauntlet to be run as far as his own room. Pride forced him to open the door of the General Office and smile at the flurry of turned heads.

"No indiscretions, kiddies. Momma'll be back."

Whether or not they believed it, they made things easy for him. A youngster with fair sideburns and a suede jacket pulled him aside.

"Screw Dunn and screw the constabulary. You want that job done, you name the time."

The smile was beginning to hurt. "There isn't any job, Jerry. The story just got tapped on the head. Thanks, anyway."

He walked the last few yards to the end of the passage. Both women were over by the window. They swung round as the door opened. His secretary's eyes and nose were red. She seemed to have shrunk since the last time he'd seen her. Shrunk and the color washed right out of her. Wanda still had her coat on. The Alice-band made her touchingly young. She stood silent, searching his face as he came towards them. Looking at her, he knew that the barriers were finally down between them.

"You heard?" He went on from need, not waiting to hear the answer. "Suspended. Dunn's flying over to make sure the place is properly disinfected." He took her portrait from his desk, gathered a few more personal belongings and stowed them in a canvas bag.

He hugged his secretary roughly, repeating what he'd said before.

"Keep your pencils sharpened, Ginny. I'll be back." He glanced round the room as if he secretly doubted it.

Wanda moved quickly, locking her arm under his. "Come on, darling."

Downstairs, they stood together just inside the entrance. The noon rush was streaming from the neighboring offices. Neither seemed to want to speak. His brain chased one thought after another without grasping any. He felt Wanda tugging at his sleeve and faced her.

111

"I love you," she said again quietly.

He nodded. "By the time Dunn gets here, we're going to be lying in the sun, somewhere in the Bahamas. He's going to learn that he can't do without me. Can you take a vacation now?"

Her eyes were puzzled. "Now? I suppose so. But what about Kowarski?"

"I meant *after* all that. When are you seeing him?" The idea of lying on a beach while Dunn trod the quarterdeck appealed to him.

Her head moved eagerly, hair swinging. "I'm having dinner with him at his home tonight. He's going to tell me what he wants us to do. The factory's in Rainham. We'll have to get down there."

"I'll hire a car." He picked a speck of dried blood from his cheek. By tomorrow night Korwin would know he's been jobbed. If Kowarski was the man Wanda said he was, he might be willing to keep the communication channel open. Even finance the escape at some later date. One thing was certain. The professional rescue teams operating out of West Berlin needed more than four days' notice. He imagined Smith's face when he heard the news — *Korwin's in West Berlin*. A rejected agent was a dangerous one. "I'd better cut, darling," he said to her. "I've a lot to do. I'll see you as soon as I can in the morning — say twelve noon, at home. I don't want you in court."

She showed no sign of surprise. "Well don't forget the doctor at three. You've got the address."

He touched her cheek with his lips. There was no point in telling her that he had no intention of going near the place. There were too many other things to do — things more important than a session with a headshrinker. If the magistrate doubled the fine, too bad.

He watched her hurry away, tall and elegant in her tailored coat.

He rode the subway to Sloane Square. It was past one when he surfaced. He bought both afternoon newspapers, scanning the court reports. There was no mention of his own case. The wind had veered to the east, peaking the faces of the passing pedestrians. He walked quickly towards the river. If anyone was on his tail he'd be leading them where they had been before.

His car was still parked in front of the apartment building. The wind and the rain had plastered it with dirt blotches. He let himself into his apartment like a burglar. The curtains were drawn. He stood quite still in the darkened hall, imagining how the scene must have been the night before. The Fate Sisters had prevented him from taking his car. It was three miles to Charing Cross — a little more to a church he had never known existed. And nothing — not even the feel of home — gave him a clue how he had gotten there. He picked a couple of letters from the mat and let daylight into the sitting room. The letters were bills. He went round the flat, straightening chairs, collecting glasses. No more than a dribble of scotch was in the bottle. He counted seven dead cans of beer and shuddered. The mixture was calculated to put you in your coffin, let alone a house of correction.

He picked the two sixpenny pieces from the tray, weighing them in his hand as he looked at the telephone speculatively.

A couple of months before, his phone had been out of order. A repair crew arrived. He had watched curiously as one of the men dialed three digits. A recorded voice answered

"Testing! Testing!" The post-office engineer had explained. The testing recording was linked to each number on the exchange. Hunter had pressed him. Could *two* recording devices be hooked to a number at the same time. The man's answer was definite — no.

Hunter lifted the receiver and dialed the testing number. A dead flat silence sounded in the earphone. He put the set back slowly and went into the bedroom smiling. He added the two sixpenny pieces to the others in the pinch-bottle.

Benjamin du Sautoy-Smith

22 February 1967

THE FOUR PRINTS were still sticky from the bath. He spread them out on his desk in the order of taking. The first showed a group of four people standing in the lobby outside the courtroom. Benstead, Hunter, the lawyer and a woman. The second had Benstead, Hunter and the woman walking towards the camera. The third was of Hunter and the woman entering the *Quest* building. The last was a shot of Hunter alone, buying a newspaper.

He put the prints back in their envelopes. Twelve hours had produced information about Hunter that was less than he'd hoped for. A work-history covering the last eight years — a record of his movements in and out of the country. It seemed that he paid his bills, had a second cousin working in the office of the High Commissioner for Canada and slept with the woman in the photograph. She was Countess Wanda Yampolska, secretary at a Polish club. The Aliens Office file on her father was routine — an ex-Polish Army Officer who had refused British citizenship. The Special Branch had nothing on either of them.

He touched a buzzer on the desk and spoke into the intercom. "Is the D.D. in, Max? OK — let me know when he is. I'll either be here or in the Annex."

He locked Hunter's file in a drawer and picked up the photographs. The french windows opened on steps leading down to the garden. Young grass glistened between the flower beds. The first crocuses were out, bright yellow under the budding spread of the elm trees. He'd carried the same bulbs home. Curious that they had rotted in their pots while these had taken.

He made his way down the path between high brick walls. He was wearing the same cavalry-twill trousers and jacket, a checked shirt and brown brogues. He opened the door at the end of the garden, still thinking about the crocuses. The scene in front of him was even sadder by daylight. Weeds flourished instead of flowers, flattened where stray cats had hunted in the undergrowth. Dark matted heaps of leaves lay as the wind had swept them. The boards nailed across the windows were bleached and discolored.

He let himself into the concrete bomb shelter. A naked light dangled on a piece of cord just inside. There were half a dozen bunks. A rusted bicycle with flat tires was propped against the wall. He made his way along a brick-lined passage to a blast-proof door. He used another key and stepped into a warm, lighted basement. Hats, coats and umbrellas hung from hooks. There were a couple of basket-chairs, a table with magazines. He ran up the stairs. The hall was bright with fluorescent strips. Steel shutters sealed the windows hermetically. The power and telephone lines ran underneath the two gardens, tapping those in the house behind. The air-conditioning system had its vents in the chimney-stacks. A dozen people worked here, day and night, unseen and un-heard by anyone outside.

He rapped lightly on a door and entered. Wooden shelves covered three of the walls from floor to ceiling. Most of the remaining space was taken by a desk and chairs. Smith closed the door carefully. People in the Annex were noise-con-scious.

He nodded at the man sitting at the desk and dropped the envelope of photographs in front of him.

"A little job for you, Lieutenant. How many of these characters do you know, if any?"

He sat down, watching the other man closely. Owen's talent wasn't unique. There were a couple of Remem-brancers working over in the Passport Office. Men with the gift of complete visual recall. Their minds stored the mem-ory of faces as other minds stored knowledge. Given a fix, they remembered.

There was little that was esoteric about the man sitting op-posite. Owen looked what he was — a junior officer in an in-fantry regiment seconded for special duty. A little over-weight perhaps, with black hair and the battered nose of a boxer. But the eyes belonged to an owl — round and un-blinking.

He held up each print, palms against the edges, studying them intensely. It seemed a long time before he answered. His voice was positive, the accent uncompromisingly Welsh.

"Two."

Smith stiffened a little. "Which two?"

Owen was holding the prints like a blackjack hand. He dealt two of them on the desk, glossy side upwards. Hunter,

117

Benstead and the woman. Hunter and the woman. His finger touched Benstead's figure.

"We've got this one on a standard take. That I'm sure about. And, I think, on a press card. I can't remember his name."

Smith nodded, wetting his lips. "And the other?"

Once on his feet, Owen was shorter than he appeared. Stolid, dressed in nondescript clothes and a rugby-club tie. He considered his shelves before using a stepladder. He pulled a manila envelope from overhead and blew dust from it. Back at the desk, he shook out a sheaf of 10 x 8 prints. He separated two and laid them before Smith.

A powerful lens had recorded a hawk-faced man standing at the foot of a gangway. Behind him was a white-painted ship with Gdynia registration. Smith remembered the photograph well. What he hadn't remembered was the woman standing in the foreground, face half-turned from the camera — Countess Yampolska. The second picture showed a bearded man in dark glasses, wearing a flower in the buttonhole of his jacket. This time the Countess was in clear focus, dressed in a brown summer frock and smiling.

He kept his voice casual. "Good work, Lieutenant. May I borrow these?"

Owen grinned, a golfer who has just shot a birdie before a critical audience. He shoved a pad and pencil at Smith.

"Sign there and you do what you like with them."

Smith scribbled his initials. "Thanks again, Lieutenant. And watch that dust. The place is getting like a pigsty." He smiled and left the room. He was no nearer Malek, possibly, but he was suddenly nearer someone even more important.

Back in his own room, he touched the buzzer again. The quiet dry voice answered immediately.

"Five minutes, Benjy. Yes, up here."

Smith called a number on the black phone. He poked at the coals in the corner fireplace. A somber Flemish portrait hung above the mantel, the subject strangely like Smith himself. There was the same foxy head with sandy hair, the same straight enigmatic stare. He'd chosen it deliberately from the Ministry of Works warehouse. As far as he knew, no one else had noticed the likeness. It was just as well the D.D. had given him five minutes. He needed time to get his facts in proper order. An hour ago these had seemed more or less balanced. Losing Hunter through his own back door last night could have been disastrous. Luckily enough, he'd put himself right back in their hands.

It had been four o'clock in the morning when Smith heard the news of Hunter's arrest. He'd showered, dressed and drunk some tea. Then he'd walked from Kew to Whitehall under a ragged, windswept sky. By the time he reached number seventeen, he knew exactly what he intended to do. It took an hour's coaxing and arguing to find the right person in Ottawa. Another hour for Ottawa to locate the managing editor of *Quest*. The result had justified every bit of Smith's endeavor. Owen's identification of Hunter's girl friend was an unexpected dividend that tipped the balance heavily in the firm's favor.

He pulled the drawer again and collected Hunter's file. He placed both sets of photographs inside it and went upstairs.

The windows in the library were open wide. Slats of pale afternoon sunshine stretched across the deep red carpet.

Smith skirted the cat lying in the center of the room — a marmalade veteran with an ear missing and extrovert habits. This was the one room where the animal was tolerated.

The General moved from fireplace to desk. He rapped the bowl of one pipe against another and laid them down, stems pointing at Smith.

"You're an obstinate bugger, Benjy, aren't you. This Hunter business. I thought I told you to make sure there was no more trouble."

Smith put Hunter's file and the photographs on the desk. The General was wearing a dark blue suit and polka-dotted bow tie. The rasp in his voice was a danger sign.

"There isn't any trouble as far as I know, sir," Smith said guardedly. "*We* didn't put him in the police court. He managed that himself, very efficiently."

The General's finger whipped up like a weapon. "Let me tell you something else he managed to do very efficiently just two hours ago. He put a complaint in to Canada House who relayed it to the Home Office. A complaint of assault and breaking-and-entering. His claim is that in both cases the offenders were what he calls 'intelligence agents.' The Home Office has promised a full inquiry."

Smith shrugged. "That ought to be interesting, sir. What do *they* suggest we do — apologize?"

The General took a long hard look at Smith. "Have you any idea what day it is, Benjy? *Wednesday*. Four days more and the balloon goes up. Meanwhile your chaps are running round like East End thugs."

Smith pulled the cigarette box near and helped himself. "I told you, sir, I'm taking full responsibility. In the meantime I have a little news for you. I'll be seeing Hunter my-self later today. There are a couple of arguments that I haven't used yet." He tapped the top of the dossier.

The General leaned across, making every word tell. "They'd better be good, Benjy, because I've a little news for you, too. Confirmed as of this morning — an Embassy signal from Warsaw — Malek escaped from prison five months ago."

Smith closed the box of matches. His hunch had been right. He laid the photographs out in two rows, the ones taken that day furthest from the General. He pinned the picture of the dockside farewell with his forefinger. He was careful to keep all sound of triumph from his voice.

"Piotr Koski alias Pierre Mathieu alias Serge Orloff. Member of the Polish Army show-jumping team and number four in their deuxième bureau. At the moment he's in Tokyo. The lady with him in the picture is a friend of Hunter's — a *close* friend."

The bridge of the General's spectacles had been mended with fuse-wire. The frames hung lopsidedly so that he had to tilt his head to focus. He studied the court shots briefly before fixing on the photograph of the man with the carnation.

"Who's this beauty?"

Smith took his time. The role of expositor pleased him. "That's a Mr. Adam Polanski, sir. Chief of the Polish Peoples Republic Purchasing Commission in this country."

The General whipped off his spectacles. "You've got some-one on him, of course?"

Smith shook his head. "You made it clear, if you remember, at a briefing last month — no permanent surveillance of

121

persons holding diplomatic passports without express orders. Polanski *has* a diplomatic passport and I haven't had any orders. Am I to take it that I do now, sir?"

"Come off it, Benjy," the General said quietly. "Slap a round-the-clock watch on the bugger — the woman too."

Smith smiled bleakly. "I already have."

The General took a turn along the carpet, hands clasped behind his back. He stepped neatly over the sleeping cat and swung round.

"Who is *she?*"

"Countess Wanda Yampolska," said Smith. "Convent-bred, aristocratic family. It would be difficult to find anyone more unlikely on the opposition's team. There's no question about her importance. These pictures prove it. Both men are active."

The General went back to his pacing, talking as he went. "And Hunter — where does he fit in?"

The answer had troubled Smith ever since he had left the Annex. He said what he believed to be the truth.

"He just doesn't know. He's the man with his finger in the crack of the door. My guess is that the woman's waiting to slam it on him."

The General pivoted in front of the fireplace. "And you'll be delighted. You're a hard man, Benjy."

Smith brought his feet together, considering the tips of his shoes. "Am I? I've never thought about it, sir. All I know is that I dislike journalists, drunks, crusaders — people who chuck their weight about. When I come up against a chap who embodies all four things, the hair rises on the back of my neck. When I find out that he's cohabiting with an opposition agent, I'm ready to bite."

122

"*Cohabiting,* Benjy? I don't know where you hear these words." The buzzer on the desk sounded. The General bent his ear to the box. He looked up.

"It's your chess player — he's waiting downstairs."

Smith gathered the file and the photographs. "Talking about likes and dislikes, you've never seen Benstead but you're not exactly enthusiastic about him, are you, sir?"

The General was staring through the open window at the sparrows raiding the bird-bowl below. His answer was vague — as if he'd almost forgotten what they were talking about.

" 'A hair perhaps divides the false and true.' The *Rubáiyát,* Benjy, fortieth stanza. You dislike journalists. I mistrust chess players. Their minds are too rigid. Have you any objection to me listening in to the interview?"

Smith grinned. "You would in any case, sir. By the way, I wanted to tell you — Berlin is on crash standby for Sunday. I'm expecting Moncrieff to fly over tomorrow. I thought you might want someone from the Home Office in on the conference."

The General lifted the cat onto his desk. "I take it you're going to have something to show them. I'm just thankful that the Director's in Washington."

Smith's smile was thin. "I'll have something, sir."

The General's gentle fingers found the cat's battered ear. It closed its eyes, leaning hard into the fondling.

"I'll be here till six. At home after that. I'll expect you to phone me the minute you have news."

He detached the silver watch from its chain and laid it in front of him. He opened a drawer and tripped a switch operating the microphone downstairs. A hidden speaker crackled. There was the sound of heavy breathing.

123

The General grunted. "Asthmatic. Probably smokes too much."

"Perhaps it's something to do with his rigid mind, sir," Smith said straight-faced. Benstead was standing in front of the french windows. He was still wearing the mustard-colored tweed suit and sagging woolen waistcoat. He turned round slowly.

Like a heron, thought Smith. One leg in the air in a foot of marsh-water and Benstead would be invisible. He dropped Hunter's file in the drawer, leaving the envelope of photographs on the top of the desk.

"Sit down, Stanley. You look whacked. What's the matter, no sleep?"

Benstead lowered himself carefully. The gesture was mechanical. A dive into his waistcoat pocket, a pastille plucked from the snuffbox. "Six hours. At my age it's enough."

Smith's nose wrinkled. It was two hours more than he'd had himself.

"I wish you'd change your brand of pills. Those bloody things make you stink like a dentist. What happened this morning? Don't worry about the court bit — I know all that. What did Hunter *say?*"

Benstead found the end of his nose with a finger. He rubbed at it gently.

"He said, 'Thank you, Stanley. I was dead-drunk last night. You got up at seven o'clock, located me in a police cell and provided a lawyer. You're a true friend and I'd trust you about as far as I could throw you.' That's what he *meant* to say, at least. Not one word about Korwin or anything connected with him."

Smith's pencil obliterated the doodling on the envelope.

He took out the sheaf of photographs. Polanski's picture lay uppermost. He whipped it quickly to the bottom of the deck, riffed through for the shot of the group in the court lobby.

"A good composition, I thought. Everyone looking quite distinguished. Everyone except Hunter, that is. How well do you know the Countess, Stanley?"

Creped lids hid Benstead's eyes for a fraction of a second. He crossed his legs, showing odd socks.

"I met her for the first time this morning. Hunter's office gave me her telephone number."

Smith swept the pictures into the open drawer. "What did you make of her?"

Benstead leaned his head on the back of his chair. He spoke, looking up at the ceiling.

"First of all she's intelligent," he said judiciously. "Very, very cool and quite sure that Hunter's in love with her."

"And how about her — is she in love with him?"

Benstead wheezed suddenly, putting his hand to his mouth. Liver-colored spots blotched the skin over his fist.

"Let's say she's concerned about him. I wouldn't go further than that. My knowledge of love is limited."

" 'A hair perhaps divides the false and true,' " quoted Smith. He was unable to resist the sally, conscious of the open microphone. "The *Rubáiyát,* stanza forty. Anyway, you left them together. When are you supposed to see him again?"

"Tomorrow," Benstead answered. "He may call me to-night. I had the impression he thinks his line is tapped."

"He reads too much of his own stuff," Smith said easily. Perhaps the General was right about Benstead after all but for a more basic reason than he'd suggested. Benstead was getting old. It was as simple as that. Without help, the Fleet

125

Street image would deflate overnight and then what — chess and a bedsitter in Islington. He spoke with rare impulsiveness.

"Have you ever thought about the country, Stanley? A job at the College, for instance?"

Benstead offered his long-toothed smile. "You mean taking classes in armed and unarmed combat — Trades-craft courses, instruction in Field Security. My varicose veins excised and with plastic arteries. No, never."

Smith unbuttoned his jacket, frowning. So much for *that* exercise in charity.

"As librarian," he said shortly. "Let's get back to Hunter. I don't care what he says any more. What concerns me is what he does. And you're in the best position to tell me."

Benstead's long face was quizzical. "I'd have thought the Countess could give me a furlong in a mile and win that one, hands down."

"No doubt. If she happened to be on our side." Something in the other man's eyes made him add: "I'm assuming that she's on *Hunter's* side. No, Stanley, you're my front-runner. I want you in court in the morning. In any case I'll be in touch with you."

Benstead collected his ulster from the sofa. He stood at the windows, fascinated by the giant stone lion on the lawn.

"I've always wondered how they got that thing in here," he said curiously and then turned. "Do you want to know if Hunter calls me?"

Smith shook his head. "I already will." He came as far as the hall with Benstead, watched the messenger close the street door. Then he went back to his desk and spoke into the intercom.

"Everything all right up there, sir?"

The General's voice was testy. "Keep that bugger out of West Willow, Benjy, even as librarian. I still don't like him."

Smith grinned. The box went dead. He went through the french windows again, down the path to the door in the wall. He made his way through the tunnel to the basement. A soldier in battle-dress was sitting in a chair outside the Code Room. He switched the service Webley to his left hand, saluted with the other.

Smith went in, ears popping with the noise from the humming dynamo. Set against the cork-lined wall was a panel the size of a large blackboard. Needles quivered on twenty dials. A maze of shortwave radio equipment covered the long metal table. Switches, tuning knobs, half a dozen microphones. The man sitting there removed his headset.

"Yessir."

Smith rattled his fingers in his ears. The hum persisted. "What have you got on that Flaxman number, Sergeant?"

The man touched a switch, stilling the auxiliary dynamo.

"I haven't checked for the last half hour, sir. But the sound's been pretty clear. We're recording from G.P.O. tape." He flicked a button. The spools on a tape machine started to revolve.

Smith cleared a chair and sat down. He leaned forward, unconscious of the smoldering cigarette in his fingers. There was the sound of a phone ringing, then Hunter's voice. "Hamish Hunter. Put me through to Mr. Burns, please." Pause. A door slammed. Then another voice, the accent pleasantly Canadian. "Hamish! What can I do for you?"

The radio operator adjusted a control. The rest of the conversation told Smith what he already knew. Hunter's complaint was completely unemotional. It was almost as though he were relating events that had happened to somebody else. His confidant promised immediate action. The tape continued to unwind with no sound except the constant ringing of a telephone.

"Can't you speed that up?" Smith asked impatiently.

The operator explained. "These are just unanswered calls, sir. He kept trying, one after another. I checked the numbers with the Post Office engineers. One's the Fulham number — the others Canonbury."

Smith left the slip of paper where it was. Fulham was his girl friend — Canonbury was Islington — Benstead, probably. The tape machine was suddenly strident. A brass band blared out a rendering of Colonel Bogey.

The sergeant had difficulty keeping the grin from his face. "He's got a sense of humor, sir."

Smith's own smile was wry. "Anything on the Fulham number?"

The man shook his head. "Just the Chelsea tone ringing. Otherwise not a peep. Nothing on the other one either."

Smith rose. "I want those three numbers monitored till further instructions."

The dynamo was humming again as he left the room. He found himself shutting the garden gate harder than usual. The strains of Colonel Bogey persisted in his ears, the age-old soldier's insult well remembered. A hard man, the General had said. And in his own flamboyant way so was Hunter. The test would be who cracked first. He ran up the steps to his room, conscious that he was being observed from the library above. The gilt clock on the mantel tinkled softly. Five o'clock. He was almost in the hall when he turned back.

He unlocked the drawer in his desk and put dossier and photographs in his briefcase.

He walked as far as the Strand, beating the home-bound charge for a bus by ten minutes. The upper deck was practically empty. It was months since he had used a bus. He sat up front, perched above the driver. He fumbled for a cigarette, looking up at the *Quest* building. Lights still blazed on the top floor. The Fourth Estate was still at it even with their bureau chief suspended — busily prying and distorting fact. Tread on their bloody toes and half a dozen lobbyists in the House were up bawling "A Free Press!" As if a press kept solvent by advertising revenue could be free.

He dropped the spent match neatly in a receptacle. Funny the way people in a bus looked out whereas those they watched rarely glanced at a bus. He alighted on the King's Road, an anonymous figure in dark blue overcoat and bowler hat. He loathed Chelsea. Girls looking like boys — boys looking like girls. Uhlan uniforms and miniskirts over bloomers. He loathed its coffee bars and mod boutiques, the pretentious louts neighing at one another in saloon bars, chits of girls looking like anemic Alices-in-Wonderland. A Hollywood cigar and an E-type Jaguar would buy the lot of them. He walked down Flood Street towards the river, alert now like a fox about to raid a hen roost. He turned left at the bottom of the street.

The small apartment-block lay beyond a patch of green behind railings. A G.P.O. repair van was parked near the triangle, covering the front and rear of the building. Trestles cordoned off a piece of pavement. An iron cover had been pulled up. A couple of workmen in overalls were doing something with wires in the hole. He strolled unobtrusively to the blind side of the van. He lifted his umbrella, a man asking the way.

"Is he still in there?"

The man in the cab nodded. A pair of field glasses lay in his lap.

"Posted a couple of letters at seven past three," he said laconically. "No visitors."

Smith lowered his umbrella. "Who takes over from you?"

The man looked at his watch. "Parrish and that new chap — I don't know his name. Buck teeth and fair hair. They're due at six in the Ajax van."

"Watch that back entrance to the Embankment," Smith warned. "I don't want to lose him a second time. I'm going in now. Keep your eyes open."

He came round from behind the vehicle, in view of Hunter's windows again. The next watch would be a cold one and long. Twelve hours in an unheated removal van. Six spyholes were concealed in the bodywork. Parrish was the sort of chap who'd remember thermoses.

The dirty blue convertible that stood in the forecourt was Hunter's. The numbers tallied with those supplied by the licensing authorities. He wiped his feet methodically on a mat stenciled BLAKE HOUSE. It was warm in the hall. The carpet on the stairs was well brushed. The potted plants were watered. A smell of burned toast came from upstairs — the tinkling theme of a children's television program. He pressed his thumb firmly on the bell-push. Hunter's answering shout was muffled as if he were some distance away.

"Who is it?"

Smith put his mouth to the mail-flap. "Me. May I come in?"

There was a long pause before the door finally opened. Hunter was in pajamas and slippers. His gray-brown hair was wild.

"What the hell are *you* peddling?" he asked belligerently. "Copies of *The Burglar's Manual*? Why didn't you use your keys. They worked before!"

Smith stepped past quickly. He hung his hat and coat on the hallstand.

"Close the door," he said quietly. "I want to talk to you."

Hunter shut the door and leaned against it, shaking his head. "*You* want to talk? You know something, Smithy. You're beginning to bug me. Now put your hat and coat back on like a good fellow and blow. That's Canadian for shove!"

Smith straddled his legs. He held himself loosely, the briefcase dangling in front of him. Things had started precisely as he'd expected.

"We're alone," he said steadily. "There's no one to impress but me and I'm immune. I came here to talk and that's what we're going to do. No brawls, no broken furniture. Just talk."

Hunter's eyes challenged for a moment. He pushed by and threw a door open. His grin dragged deep lines from nose to mouth.

"OK, we'll talk."

"Thank you." Like a vicarage tea party, thought Smith. He walked into the big room. An adjustable bracket lamp was lit on the long table. There was paper in the typewriter, more beside it. A pleasant room, Smith decided. With gay prints, icons, a couple of press pictures of a steeplechase finish. He took a chair, sitting with his back to the window. The man in the van would be able to pick him out easily. No

131

sense in taking a chance with someone in Hunter's position.

The Canadian went into the kitchen. He returned carrying a can of beer and one glass. He poured the beer expertly, drank and wiped his mouth on his pajama sleeve.

"OK. I'm listening."

Smith's eye caught the record player. A brightly colored jacket lay on top of it. *The Bridge Over the River Kwai — The Original Sound-Track.* He took out Hunter's file and put the briefcase on the floor at his feet.

"I know a little more about you than I did last night," he started conversationally. "Clergyman's son. Oddly enough, so was I. Brilliant school record — there you have me. I could never learn anything."

Hunter poured the rest of the beer. "You haven't changed. Suppose we skip what you know about me. I'm doing my best to find out a little about you. I've got a strange feeling I just might make it." His eyes flicked sideways at the typewriter.

"Free-lance work?" Smith asked pleasantly. Muscles hardened in Hunter's jawline. Smith continued. "Please let me finish. You're ambitious, unmarried and at this particular moment you're in about as big a mess as you could be. I'm here to help you get out of it. Not because I like you. Because it's expedient."

Hunter's plume of toffee-gray hair nodded. "I've been waiting for that word ever since I met you. What are you going to do, have me worked over again?"

Smith went on patiently. "You came back from Warsaw with information that's of concern to this country. You were asked to get it to the right people. All right, you did. I'll take full responsibility for what happened next. I made the

132

wrong decision. The reasons are unimportant now. Korwin's life *is* important. We've only got three days."

The Canadian fetched another can of beer. He poured it with a suggestion of defiance.

"You sounded just as plausible last night. 'The fact is, you've been *had*, Hunter!' I wasn't then and I don't intend to be now."

Smith nodded heavily. "So your friend's children are almost certainly going to die because Mr. Hunter's feelings have been wounded. Is that it?"

Hunter smiled, a conjuror producing a rabbit from a hat. "Not quite, no. You see nobody's *going* to die. There won't be any explosions and nobody waiting in East Berlin. Korwin and the others will work things out their own way."

Caution flooded Smith's brain. It was unlikely that Hunter had found a way of contacting Warsaw. Likelier that someone had promised to help him. The woman and Polanski. The inference was alarming. Hunter was ripe for the right approach from someone who sounded convincing. And who more convincing than the woman he associated with. If Hunter believed her, it was a matter of time before Malek's location and alias were in the Warsaw authorities' hands. He did his best to reach beyond the stubborn mask facing him.

"I want Korwin, Hunter. I'll give you my word that the three of them will be picked up. I've already made arrangements. More than that, I'll give you a story and clearance for it, one that will get you your job back."

Hunter's face tightened dangerously. "I don't need you to get my job back, Smith. And I've *got* a story. All about betrayal and extortion. And you're the central character. I'll give you two minutes to get out of here. That's two more than you're worth." He stood up.

Smith gathered his briefcase. For the second time in two days he had fallen flat on his face. The General wasn't going to like it. There was only one way left of dealing with Hunter — a surveillance so tight that he wouldn't be able to breathe without Smith's knowing. Hunter had to make his move soon. He was governed by the same urgency as everyone else. When he made his move, the woman and Polanski would be there to help him. So much the better.

He collected his hat and coat from the hallstand. Hunter stood watching from the half-open door, his mouth set in hard lines.

"You're wrong," Smith said, shaking his head.

The Canadian shrugged. "I'll live with it if I am."

"If you change your mind . . ." Smith started.

Hunter shook his head. "I won't. And don't worry about my hurt feelings. I'm a resilient sort of guy." He slammed the door, just missing Smith's leg.

Stanley Dangerfield Benstead

22 February 1967

HE PAID OFF the cab on the corner and stood for a while looking in the windows of a radio store. The same face showed on half a dozen television screens, soundlessly announcing the six o'clock news. Traffic rumbled along the Charing Cross Road, a couple of blocks away. On the opposite side of the street, an attendant was shifting a billboard in the lobby of the theater.

Benstead turned and walked slowly towards Leicester Square. A succession of brightly lit windows offered a dubious display of fetish footwear, "Gay Gear," cheap transistors and a jumble of Hong Kong junk-jewelry.

The dingy office building on the corner had three entrances. One on each side street, the other in the right angle of the triangle. He used the nearest, entering the shabby lobby behind the elevator shaft. A couple of sad lights burned near the front door. Another door marked INQUIRIES was closed and padlocked. A name-board hung on the wall. The space next to the sixth floor was empty. He waited for a while, assuring himself that the lobby was empty. The front entrance remained open till midnight for the benefit of the few people who lived in the building. A linoleum-covered stairway behind the elevator ascended into darkness.

He crossed the lobby and pushed his hand through a slit in one of the mailboxes. The key had been taken. He started up the stairs, resting for a second on each landing. A door opened as he reached the fifth floor. A dog barked. A straw-blond in stretch-pants appeared in the passage, carrying a dachshund. Her eyes sought and then dismissed him. The cage rattled down leaving the odor of cheap scent behind. The sixth floor was shaped like a triangle, office doors opening off the exterior sides. A billhead was pinned to one of the doors. FRIENDSHIP PRESS. He turned the handle. The lock sprung closed behind him.

The blind had been lowered on the one window. Cartons of pamphlets were stacked wherever there was room. The walls were bare save for a Polish National Airline calendar. There was dust everywhere and no telephone. Polanski was warming his legs in front of a small electric heater.

Benstead sat down tiredly, hands on his knees, waiting for the pain to ease in his chest. Polanski's poised elegance made him feel old and hopeless. His breathing gradually became normal. He lifted his head.

"You understood the message?"

Polanski's hands were expressive. "Part of it. I would think you are right about the surveillance. I took the necessary precautions. We can be sure that I wasn't followed here. The part about Yampolska, I didn't understand."

A cistern flushed on the floor below. Benstead leaned forward. "I was called in by Smith. He showed me a picture they'd taken outside the court this morning — of Hunter, the lawyer, Yampolska and myself. It was a shock production designed to test my reactions. I explained that Hunter's office had given me her telephone number. He knew her name, by the way. There were more pictures but he didn't show me any. But I did see one, before he could put it at the bottom of the pile. It was a picture of you and Yampolska taken together. The likeness was unmistakable."

Polanski removed his spectacles. He wiped his eyes, staring at the handkerchief, and muttered something under his breath. Then clearly.

"It is unimportant."

Benstead's tone sharpened. "I don't think you understand. This is a reconnaissance picture. It means that you are no longer just a routine security risk for them. You have moved up into the positive bracket. And you have taken her with you. Or what would be worse, vice-versa. Smith is anything but a fool. He is a professional. He *knows* that Korwin is Malek. I don't have to be told this — I sense it. He knows as much as we do, Adam. And he's waiting for the flies to come to the honey."

Polanski was smoking. He waved his cigarette holder nervously. "I too had a summons. To the Embassy. The Poznanski boy was arrested last night, driving an empty taxi. He talked before he died. The Security Militia raided the farmhouse. It was too late. Malek and the girl were gone. His arrest has become top-priority. The Commissar himself is in charge. I am recalled to Warsaw. I leave tonight. My instructions are that you will take over the field operations here. Congratulations."

The clipped sentences seemed to come from a great distance. Promotion to captain as the ship foundered on a rock. Congratulations. He rose and went to the window, drew a corner of the blind aside. Parked cars below stretched like a file of shiny beetles. He turned to face the other man.

"And *my* instructions?"

Polanski's tinted lens gave his expression inscrutability. "Hunter is meeting Yampolska tomorrow. He is taking the film with him. They will drive down to Rainham and take the back lane to Kowarski's factory. It runs alongside a reservoir for three miles. There are no houses there. Just trees and potato fields."

Benstead groped for his snuffbox, rattling it mechanically to see if it held pastilles.

"And Smith's men will be behind them."

The remark made Polanski's smile brilliant. "Undoubtedly. Look!" He swept the table free of papers and put three pencils in a line. Two close together, one some distance ahead. He touched the second pencil. "Hunter and Yampolska!" He drew a line behind it. "A wire rope stretched from one side of the lane to the other. As soon as Hunter's car passes, the rope is drawn taut, three feet from the ground. At thirty miles an hour it will sheer straight through anything following. You are waiting in the third car with Stefan. You take the road on past the factory and back onto the main London highway. The *M. V. Polonia* is berthed at Wapping. You will take the film straight there. Everything you need will be prepared ready for you."

Benstead wiped the stickiness from his lips. A basic ingredient seemed to be missing from the plan.

"What about Hunter and the woman?"

Polanski spoke like a man remembering something unpleasant that happened to a friend.

138

"They crashed," he said simply. "They hit the reservoir wall at sixty miles an hour. One never knew why. A skid, perhaps. Nerves. Possibly Hunter had been drinking. You will decide. She has been told that your authority is complete. She will do whatever you say up to the last minute. If the plan needs adjustment, you must draw on your own initiative."

Benstead thought for a while, coughing gently. "I am too old to be used as an enforcer without being sure of an escape route. This is England, Adam, and you know my history."

Polanski whipped his spectacles from his nose. His voice was quiet and brittle.

"It has not been forgotten. You will sail on the *Polonia*. Make your arrangements accordingly. Good night and good luck." He shrugged into his coat and opened the door.

Benstead sat listening to the rickety elevator make its slow descent. He waited the customary ten minutes before locking up the office. He made his way down by the service stairs. The air outside was raw. He muffled his face in his cape and walked towards the subway station. The wind struck even colder in Islington. He took the shortest way home. The pub on the corner was open. A stale smell of beer and tobacco drifted out as he passed. The shabby row of Victorian houses faced a blank school wall. By day the street was bedlam, a shadowed place by night where the sound of a car, the tap of a woman's heels, echoed in the deserted playground. He climbed the steps wearily, avoiding the empty milk bottles, the perambulator standing in the dim hall. He waited at the foot of the stairs till a door opened on the landing above. A woman's head peered over the banisters. Rollers in her hair gave her the appearance of a piece of electronic equipment. He lifted his hat at her. She swatted the air behind as a child bawled fretfully.

"Oh, it's you, Mr. Benstead."

He nodded. "The rent. I haven't forgotten. I'll leave a check in the morning."

She hung a few inches lower. "Your phone's been ringing. What's it like outside?"

"Windy and cold. Good night, Mrs. Riley."

He opened his door, switching on the lights. His inspection was thorough. First the double-action spring lock on the door, then the windows. He drew the curtains. The furniture in the room was a mixture of comfort and ugliness. A clothes closet with an oval mirror, curly-legged table and chairs. A couch-bed ready for occupation. A second door gave access to a kitchen-bathroom. He hung his ulster near the gas geyser to dry and picked up the phone. Hunter's number replied immediately. Benstead lowered himself wearily on the end of the bed.

"I just thought I'd call to see how it went at the doctor's."

"Fine." Hunter's voice was almost jaunty. "This phone's tapped, by the way. I've been calling you — did you hear that I've been suspended?"

"I heard." Benstead answered. "It'll blow over. They need you."

Hunter's laugh was easy. "If they don't, the French and the Germans do. We'll see. Are you going to be in court in the morning, Stanley?"

"Positively," promised Benstead. "Is everything else under control?"

"Everything. Well, get a good night's sleep, Stanley." His

voice assumed the syrupy tone of a radio performer. "And good night, Mrs. Umbriago, *wherever* you are!"

Benstead replaced the receiver. He unlocked a cupboard and took out a plastic bag. He emptied a long-barreled 9-mm Parabellum onto the bed, a spare clip of shells and a silencer. He pumped a round into the breech and screwed the silencer onto the barrel. He checked the rest of the mechanism, putting the gun under his pillow. He yawned, scratching himself heartily. Hunter's mouth was too big. It was as well that it wouldn't be open much longer.

Hamish Hunter

23 February 1967

HE ATE breakfast standing in the kitchen. The clock said a quarter to nine. He had been awake since six, fresh from a ten-hour unbroken sleep. The woman would have nothing to do when she came. He had made the bed, vacuumed the floor and generally straightened up. He rinsed the few breakfast things in the sink, locked and bolted the back door.

Pale sunshine brightened the sitting room. He closed the windows. The phone had been off the hook since he'd spoken to Benstead. Wanda wouldn't move from the house till she heard from him. He'd call her from outside as soon as he'd finished in court. He stood over the table, reading the title page of his finished article. "Expedience, English-style." It was a long way from the original story. This was a straightforward piece of factual reporting. Ten thousand words that covered the events of the past three days. And if more was wanted he could supply it. He put the typescript in his briefcase.

He dressed quickly. Blue suit, white shirt, black shoes. He brushed his hair and smiled at himself in the mirror. Pretty for the judge. The contents of his pockets lay on the dresser. Passport, keys, driving license, money. He checked the thin

142

sheaf of bills. Twelve pounds. They might well hit him with a fine that was more than that. He slipped his checkbook inside his jacket. Briefcase and mac. Nothing forgotten.

He closed the hall door behind him and stepped into sunshine. The rain had left his car filthy. He let the top down, scouting both ends of the street. The houseman was raking the grass behind the railings. He started the motor and backed out of the forecourt. A taxi turned the corner as he drove off. He had a brief glimpse of two passengers in the driving mirror. He took the direct route to the Strand. King's Road, round behind the Palace, the Mall. The taxi was still in its place as he neared the Admiralty Arch. He swung left without warning, pulling up at the foot of the steps. The cab went through the Arch and stopped. Two men got out and separated.

Hunter slammed the door of the convertible. They were very sure of him. They hadn't even gone through the motions of paying off the cab. Either that or the taxi was a decoy. He glanced round the parking place. A crocodile-file of schoolgirls carrying cameras wound down the steps. Behind them was one of the men from the cab. Hunter picked up his briefcase and mac. By the time he'd finished with them, their feet would be giving them trouble. He crossed Trafalgar Square without a backward look. It was a quarter to ten as he reached the top of Bow Street. The court building was doubly forbidding in the sunshine. The gates were closing on a police wagon as he went up the steps. The scene in the lobby could have been yesterday's. The same brand of hard-nosed detectives with their sorry bag of culprits. The same tearful wives and mothers. Benstead was talking to the lawyer outside the probation office. The cop who'd arrested him wore a blue mac over uniform trousers and no cap. He grinned as Hunter approached. Hunter waved.

"Be with you in five minutes!"

He walked over to the waiting pair. He touched Benstead's arm and nodded at Wells.

"By the way, I didn't bother with the doctor."

The lawyer shed his look of professional blandness. "You didn't keep the appointment — but why not?"

"For two reasons, Mr. Wells," Hunter said steadily. "Neither of them concerns you any more. I'm grateful for your help but I don't need you. Have your secretary send me a bill."

The lawyer's face reddened. "As you like," he said stiffly.

Benstead watched him through the door and down the steps. "I suppose you know what you're doing," he said quietly. He wore the same battered hat and brown tweed suit. His only concession to the weather was that his ulster had been left behind.

Hunter's eyes sought the clock. Seven minutes to ten. "It's an open-and-shut case of drunk," he said deliberately. "I've had enough of being shoved around, Stanley. I need a doctor's certificate and lawyer as much as you do. I'm going to apologize humbly and pay my fine. Then you and I can talk business."

Benstead's eyes unhooded over a wary smile. "What sort of business?"

Hunter shrugged. "I'm not sure yet, Stanley. It all depends how high you are on your friend Smith. I'll talk to you about it afterwards. First let's get this over."

He strolled across the lobby to the police constable. "Are we all set?"

144

The courtroom door opened as if the usher had heard. "Hamish Hunter!"

Hunter climbed into the dock. The same red-faced jailer was on duty. Hunter ducked his head at the bench and sat down.

The clerk read from his sheet. "Hamish Hunter, Your Worship. Put back from yesterday for sentence."

The magistrate frowned, looking at the empty seat on his left. "Aren't you represented by counsel today?"

Hunter came to his feet. "No sir. Whatever's to be said I can say myself."

The magistrate glanced at his notes. "I remember the case very well. You were remanded for medical evidence to be called. Is the doctor in court?"

Hunter shook his head. Benstead's asthmatic breathing was noisy behind the dock.

"I didn't keep the appointment, sir. I didn't think it was necessary."

The magistrate's mouth compressed. "You didn't think it was necessary. I see. Don't sit down." He leaned over the bench whispering to the clerk. He straightened up, his thin voice cutting. "You're the sort of man who puts himself above the law. Not satisfied with behaving like an animal in public, you make it your business to waste the time of the court. I'm quite certain that nothing I can say would have any impression on you. This may. You'll go to prison for seven days."

Feet scraped. There was the rustle of clothing. A ring of faces seemed to close in on Hunter. He gripped the front of the dock, his voice shaking.

"You're out of your mind! I appeal against this sentence. You don't know what you're doing."

The magistrate's expression was unmoved. "Seven days on each count, the sentences to run consecutively. Next case!"

Hunter threw his arms wide, appealing to the press box. "You see what this old goat's . . ."

He choked as the jailer's forearm crooked round his throat. A cop broke Hunter's grasp on the dock rail. Another kicked the Canadian's legs from under him. He saw Benstead standing up, his mouth working as if he was trying to say something. Then he felt himself lifted and run out of the courtroom, his arms locked high between his shoulder blades. The crowd outside scattered as the flying wedge hurtled across the lobby and down the steps to the cells. Hunter stumbled through the open doorway, grabbing at the table to stop himself falling. The sound of bolts shooting home echoed along the corridor.

He sat down on the plank bed, straightening his jacket and tie. A latticed shaft of sunlight pierced the dirty barred windows. He lit a cigarette, the fingers of both hands trembling. *Two weeks' imprisonment!* It couldn't be true. They'd be down after a while. As soon as the business of the court had finished probably. He heard the magistrate's voice, harsh with authority. *I hope that you've learned your lesson, Hunter, I'm varying this sentence to a fine.*

He blew smoke nervously. That might take hours and meanwhile Wanda was waiting. The cottage was fifty miles away. He had to talk to her — at least send a message. He went to the door. He lowered his lifted hand, thinking better of it. Christ, no, no banging. He pressed the bell gently. A marker fell outside indicating the source of the summons. Nothing happened. He put his ear against the crack in the

146

door. Water was dripping in the recess. The buzz of the bell died in empty silence. He tried again, keeping his finger pressed firmly on the button. Still no answer. He sat down, forcing himself to be calm. He looked at his watch. Twenty minutes past ten. That couldn't be right. The spring was fully wound. The second hand ticked methodically.

It was a quarter of an hour before the gate clanged at the bottom of the stairs. He was on his feet waiting when the door opened. It was the same cop who had been on cell duty the day before. Benstead was behind him. The cop shook his head at Hunter, his eyes puzzled.

"You must like it, mate. OK. You've got five minutes." He removed himself a couple of yards and leaned against the wall, whistling.

Hunter was standing in the doorway. "What's this *mean,* Stanley? He wants an apology, right?"

Benstead smoothed invisible hair on his bald scalp, his face troubled.

"It means you've just talked yourself into fourteen days' imprisonment. They say you can't appeal — at least against your conviction. You pleaded guilty. Against your sentence I'm not sure. *He* won't give you bail, that's certain. I spoke to the probation officer. It'll be next week before we could get you in front of judge-in-chambers. Are you satisfied?"

A hot wave of anger surged. The cop turned his head as it sounded in Hunter's voice.

"Look, Stanley — don't *you* start riding me!"

Benstead's voice was controlled. "*Think,* Hamish. Time's short. Whether you believe it or not, I'm on your side. Whatever you want me to do, I'll do. Is that understood?"

147

Hunter searched the other's face. Tired eyes stared back compassionately. But compassion wasn't enough. Benstead had other loyalties. Hunter shifted his feet uncertainly.

"All right, I'm going to jail. Which one?"

Benstead glanced behind at the cop. The man shrugged. "Brixton. He's a first offender and they want cleaners."

"Brixton," Hunter repeated. They might as well have said Dartmoor. "Then you tell Wanda to go there immediately. Tell her to see the Governor. I've got to talk to her."

The cop broke in. "She'd be wasting her time. You're a convicted prisoner. You got to *earn* visiting privileges. Two weeks isn't enough for your name to dry. Under a month you earn nothing. One reception letter and that's your lot. Your best bet is to tell your friend what you want the lady to know."

Nobody spoke. Then Benstead looked past Hunter at the briefcase lying on the bed.

"If there's anything you want her to have — I'm sure there'd be no objection."

The cop yawned indifferently. "I didn't see anything," he said pointedly. "Just make your minds up. The sergeant said five minutes."

Instinct told Hunter that Benstead believed that the briefcase held what Smith wanted. The thought decided him. He answered deliberately.

"Just get hold of Wanda. And tell her to do what I said."

Benstead's long head nodded. "I'll do that, Hamish. And don't worry. We'll have you out on Monday on appeal if it's humanly possible."

The door closed again. Hunter stood with his ear to the

148

crack till the footsteps died at the end of the corridor. He unfastened his briefcase and ripped the typescript in pieces. He flushed the fragments down the lavatory bowl. They'd search him in jail. For all he knew, they might send everything he had on him to Smith. One thing they couldn't do — read his mind. The next time he wrote the piece, there'd be fresh material to add.

He sat down, lighting another cigarette. The pack was only half full. He'd have to ask the cop whether they smoked in English jails. Maybe you had to rob a bank before you earned that privilege. He leaned his head in his hands, remembering Wanda's expression when he first told her about Korwin. Her look of disbelief as he'd evaded her questions. There were no divided loyalties *there*. He'd been a fool not to trust her entirely. Alone he'd achieved nothing. *She'd* found the means of sending the message. It was almost a relief to realize that the initiative must pass to someone else. She'd get in to see him — he was sure of it. He had a vague picture of a screen between them — her face dim beyond it. There'd be somebody listening. No matter. He only had two things to tell her. First, where the film was. This could be done casually — a throwaway line that would register. And she had to know that she'd be followed. Once she knew, she'd find a way to shake whoever was on her tail.

The hours passed, the only break a meal Benstead had sent in from a nearby cafe. It was gone three when a cell door opened along the corridor. He heard voices, the shuffle of retreating footsteps. Then his own lock was sprung. The young cop grinned at him.

"The carriage awaits. And mind what I say, mate. Behave yourself in there. They're a lot rougher than we are."

149

Hunter picked up his briefcase and mac. The afternoon sun shone at the far end of the corridor. He walked towards it. Outside, a Black Maria was backed up against the entrance, its rear doors wide. Strategically placed cops blocked any dash for the street beyond the wide-flung gates. He climbed the two steps into the vehicle. A central passage was lined on both sides with steel cubicles. The waiting cop ushered him into one of them and turned the handle. There was barely room to stand. A metal seat faced the front. A tiny pane of opaque glass let in a semblance of light. At the top of the door was a stout grill. By putting his cheek flat against it, he could just see through the rear window. A cop standing on the steps lifted his hand. Hunter sat down hard as the vehicle lurched through the gates. Over his head was what looked like an escape hatch. He pushed it tentatively. Locks controlled from the cab held it fast. He felt the van turn left, the bodywork shuddering as the driver changed gear. The graffiti scratched on the wall were short of lyrical. Names, dates and sentences. One wag had scribbled *Georgie Jacobs loves the Lord Chief Justice.*

He lit another cigarette. Seven left. He should have asked Benstead to send some in. A mincing voice called from the door opposite.

"How long you in for, dear? Three months, me. Imagine — three months and all those lovely burglars! I can't wait to have me ball-and-chain put on!"

Reality slipped away through the back window. The rise and fall of Westminster Bridge. Darkness as they lumbered under Waterloo Viaduct. The board outside Kennington Public Baths.

ALBERT GEE V PADDY MC GUIRE
(*Battersea*)   (*Liverpool*)

Children racing down the long slope of Brixton Hill, swinging school satchels. The van turned into a side street. It followed a twenty-feet-high wall for a quarter of a mile. Giant studded gates swung open, trapping the van inside a courtyard. More gates, but barred this time instead of solid. The van stopped. One of the two cops unlocked the cubicles, one left, one right, kicking the doors shut as the occupants climbed out.

Four-tier cell blocks towered above the administration offices. The exercise yards were paved with concentric rings of concrete. Freedom lay beyond the sweep of wall that blocked the view on all sides. The van had parked in front of a one-story building. Hunter went through a door marked RECEPTION. On the left of the short length of passage a warder was standing behind a desk with a strong light hanging over it. The prisoners were sitting on a bench facing him. One of the cops who had ridden the wagon tossed a batch of committal papers on the desk. His voice was entirely impersonal. He might well have been delivering the week's groceries.

"Eight, George. Six remands and two convicted."

The warder's cap was on the back of his head. His tunic was cut like the cop's. A whistle-chain drooped from his breast pocket. The side of his trousers bulged with the weight of the hidden truncheon. He wore shoulder-flashes that read H.M.P. He signed acceptance of the arrivals.

"Thank you, Harry. Nice and early tonight."

The cop picked up his papers. "Not much business today, that's why. It'll be different tomorrow. I see there's a ban-the-bomb meeting in Trafalgar Square. That's always good for five or six loads." Both men exchanged looks of resignation. The warder let the cop out and locked up behind him. He walked back to his desk and glanced from the committal papers to the eight men on the bench.

"How many of you left here this morning?"

Five hands shot up. He checked their names against the papers.

"All right, you know where to go. *Five coming down, sir!*" A voice round the corner bawled acknowledgment.

The jailer adjusted his lamp. "Which of you's Arthur Cox?"

A man in his fifties stood up, holding his hat as if he expected something to be placed in it. The jailer read from a form.

"You're committed for trial at the Inner London Sessions. Off you go, first left and keep on the matting. *Another one on, sir!*" The same voice answered.

The jailer scanned the remaining pair. "Archibald Firth?"

The man beside Hunter moved coquettishly. An inch of black showed at the roots of his ash-blond hair arrangement. He wore tight tartan trews, a reefer jacket and smelled of some exotic lotion.

"That's me, dear," he replied.

If the jailer heard, he showed no sign of it. "You were sentenced to three months' imprisonment at West London Police Court. Have you been in prison before?"

The man's eyes were round. "*Me?* In prison before? Never, dear."

The jailer's face reddened. "You did say 'dear,' didn't you?"

Firth smiled winningly. "You're not cross, are you?"

The jailer's voice was dangerous. "Say it once more and I'll put you where you can talk to yourself for three days — on a diet of bread and water. Now take yourself off and wash the lice out of your hair."

The man pantomimed disgust for Hunter's benefit and swished down the passage. The jailer picked up the last committal paper.

"Hamish Hunter." He pronounced the given name as 'Hamonish.' "You've got two sentences of seven days to run consecutively. Is this your first time inside?"

Hunter nodded. "It's the first time. How would I find out if somebody's here to see me?"

The jailer's hand froze in midair. "What do you mean, somebody here to see you?"

"A visitor — my fiancée," Hunter explained.

The jailer sucked his teeth, obviously uncertain whether or not he was being jobbed. He decided against it.

"Listen to me, dasher. This is a nick not a boarding school. People don't just walk in and out when they feel like it."

Hunter looked at him steadily. "I asked you a civil question. If you don't want to answer it, maybe I should ask the Governor."

The door slammed in the desk. "You do that," the warder said bleakly. "You'll find a rule card in your cell. Read it. It'll tell you where to get *all* the answers you want. Now pick up your things and follow the others." The same bawl announced Hunter's impending arrival.

A strip of coconut-fiber matting stretched along the brightly polished floor. Another desk was at the end of the passage — a larger one with a bull-necked warder behind it. His interview with the queer had left him uncertain of temper. A rat-faced man in prison clothing stood by his side, holding a sheet. The warder picked up a cell card. He filled in Hunter's particulars. Name. Age. Religion. Date of expiry of sentence. His offenses went on the back, the information hidden when the card would hang outside his cell. The jailer opened a cloth-bound ledger marked PROPERTY BOOK.

"Take everything out of your pockets and put it on the desk."

The trusty's eyes assessed the pack of cigarettes. The jailer tossed it into a trash basket. He entered Hunter's name in the ledger and wrote a description of the contents of his pockets.

"A passport. Eleven pounds in notes. Seven and six in coins. A bunch of keys. A comb. A yellow metal signet ring and a yellow metal watch marked 'Omega.' Is that the lot?"

"The ring and watch are gold," said Hunter.

The jailer looked up. "They're yellow metal in here." He put everything but the money into a small canvas bag and tied it with a label bearing Hunter's name and number. "Take your clothes off and give them to the orderly. Then wrap yourself in the sheet and go through the first door on your right."

Hunter undressed and covered himself with the coarse calico. Facing him were half a dozen cubicles, open at the top and with half-doors. Each held a bath, stool and duckboard.

154

A line painted nine inches from the bottom of the tub showed the allowed level of hot water. The bath was already filled. He sat down in it gingerly. Maybe Wanda had come and been turned away, too late to catch the prescribed visiting hours. In which case she'd be back in the morning. A grizzled head showed over the top of the door.

"What size shoes you take?"

"Eight," said Hunter. The soap smelled strongly of lye. The queer was caroling at the far end of the bathhouse. A pile of clothing had been draped on the door. A pair of shoes slid across the floor under it. He toweled himself and dressed. Gray trousers, battledress top, rough striped shirt and black socks ringed with red. The unpolished shoes had been around for a long while. He opened the door. The pillowcase contained two sheets, a dish-rag — a metal comb and safety-razor — a hairbrush smelling of disinfectant, a new toothbrush. A library card inside a copy of *The Girl of the Limberlost,* Bible and prayer book. He carried the bag through to the waiting room. The rest of the vanload was sitting on a bench in front of a steam radiator. The unconvicted prisoners still wore their own clothes. Firth made room for Hunter, complaining in a loud voice about his uniform.

"Trashy old gear, I call it. Not what I'm used to at all. *You* know that, dear. You saw me. Every stitch from Carnaby Street. Making you wear other people's drawers — they ought to be ashamed of themselves!"

A gate crashed open. A man in civilian clothes stalked in as if he were finishing first in a long-distance walking race. He was followed by a jailer in a white coat with a silver cross on his sleeve. They vanished through a door which opened

155

again almost immediately. The jailer crooked his finger at the first man on the bench. His instructions were loud as the door closed.

"Give your full name and number to the Medical Officer. Drop your trousers and lift up your shirt."

The room was stock-institutional. An expanse of linoleum. Another of the stand-up desks, as if the user had no time to waste sitting down. Hunter stepped on a scale. The dial was mysteriously reversed, preventing him from reading his own weight. The white-jacketed hospital warder signaled a partial disrobing. Hunter's trousers collapsed round his knees. He lifted his shirt. The doctor was still wearing his hat. He glanced up from the desk, pen poised over Hunter's cell card. A space was reserved for medical comment. His words ran into one another.

"Cough not suffering from V.D. are you general health all right good is that the lot Mr. Flanagan?"

He scribbled *A-1* on the card. The interview had lasted two minutes. The remand prisoners had been removed. A warder escorted Hunter and the queer through gates, along a covered passage into a cellblock. There were four galleries, thirty-eight cells on each. Bridges in the middle and on the ends connected the landings. Wire netting stretched across the intervening space, preventing suicide-dives from the top gallery. A voice from a cell yelled "You'll be sorry!" as they climbed to the third floor. The jailer undid two doors. He swung his keys impatiently.

"Get your water if you want it!"

Hunter put his pillowcase down in the cell. An enameled jug and washbasin stood on a scrubbed-wood stand. Underneath was a metal chamber pot. On the table, a tin knife, plate, spoon and pint-pot. He carried the jug to the recess. A half-door concealed a lavatory. Beside it was a sink with a faucet. There was a second recess on the other side of the bridge. The cells had been scientifically designed for one prisoner eight years before. Most of them now housed three. After the five o'clock lock-up there was no practical provision for the use of the lavatories. Men stored the contents of their chamber pots for the night, emptying them first thing in the morning in the recesses. The chore coincided with the serving of breakfast.

Hunter filled his jug. He walked back to his cell. The warder closed the door, rattling the outside handle. He peered through the spy-hole as if he expected Hunter to have vanished through the perforations in the ventilator cover. There was a three-tiered bunk, a chair and mirror. The lower halves of the wall were painted a bilious yellow, above that whitewashed. He made up his bed on the bottom bunk and studied the rule card. *Regulations For Convicted Prisoners. You may see any of the following by applying to your land-ing-officer when your cell is opened in the morning. The Governor, Medical Officer, Chaplain.* The list of misde-meanors was a long one. Idleness, refusal to obey an order, use of foul language, indecency. A blanket clause at the end wrapped up all unspecified peccadilloes. ". . . or in any way offend against good order and discipline." The privileges listed applied only to prisoners serving sentences of one month or more. He hung the card on the wall again. As far as he could see, anyone falling short of canonization-standard was likely to spend most of his sentence in the cooler.

Already he had lost sense of time. It was dark outside. He stood on his chair, looking out beyond the squared panes and flat bars placed laterally. Lights showed in the cellblock on the far side of the yard. Beyond that was the inevitable wall. He climbed down and started to pace from window to door. Five steps and then turn. You didn't have to be a psychopath to wind up in jail. Or even a criminal. You went about your business, day in, day out, surrounded by known values. Then the wrong word to the right man and disaster clobbered you from out of left field. In his case, Smith. The chain of events stretched from the meeting in the park to a cell in Brixton Prison.

He stopped in his tracks as someone in the cell below pounded on the ceiling. Each word was a separate snarl.

"Take — your — fucking — boots — off!"

He continued to pace in his stockinged feet. He was still walking when his door handle was tested from outside. The light went out. He stretched out on the bottom bunk, listening to the noises in the cellblock. He lay there for a long time, conscious of footsteps padding along the galleries, the furtive movement of his spy-hole.

Morning came without the clamor of the bell he expected. A jangle of keys on the bottom floor triggered movement throughout the building. Bunks were shifted, windows thrown open. He had his trousers, shirt and shoes on by the time his own door was unlocked. He carried his chamber pot out on the landing, waited his turn to empty it into the lavatory. The smell was unbearable. A jailer stood on the bridge, holding a slate and chalk. His voice lifted at intervals.

"Hurry up and shut your doors, applications bring your cards."

Hunter walked onto the bridge. "I'd like to see the Governor."

158

The jailer took his card. "You'll see him in any case. You're a reception."

The cell doors were closed to be opened again, one at a time. The jailer served breakfast from receptacles carried by orderlies. Cans of porridge and tea. A basket of eight-ounce loaves. A tray bearing half-ounce pats of margarine. A razor blade came as a bonus, to be returned at the warder's next visit. The porridge and tea was unsweetened. Hunter ate a little bread, washing it down with the dark brown brew. He shaved and folded his bedding. Then he straightened the cell, arranging the furniture after the diagram on the landing. It was nine o'clock when the block was unlocked for labor. The cons stood at their doors, waiting for the order to form up below in their respective parties. Bakers, cooks, gardeners. The boiler-house and cleaning details. Trusties working at the Front Gate and in the Administration Building. The gangs moved off. A slotted board hung outside each cell. Hunter noticed that another card had been slipped into the one by his door. It read LANDING CLEANER. He waited till a warder shouted from the floor below.

"Governor's applications and receptions! Fall in below and make sure you've got your ties on."

Hunter knotted the strip of coarse gray material. Light streamed through barred windows in the roof and enormous expanses of glass at the end of the block. He took his place in the queue downstairs. *A yard apart and no talking!* The queer was directly in front of him. Applications were taken in the Principal Officer's room. The warder stiffened as a gate opened.

"Stand to attention for the Governor!"

There was a token shuffling of feet. The Governor made

his entrance, a tall man in his sixties. He wore a dark suit and carried himself as if he expected mutiny might break out in the thin line of apprehensive prisoners. A rack-shouldered warder followed him, uniform and cap peak glittering with gold braid. The man in charge saluted.

"Five prisoners, all correct, sir!"

The Governor took the salute casually. The office door opened and shut, opened again. "First man!" The line shuffled forward as the applications were dealt with. The queer emerged with a stricken look on his face. The Chief Officer's bellow followed.

"See that man's hair is cut, short back and sides, sir!"

They seemed to use "sir" to one another in front of prisoners as if striving to set a precedent. The response was negligible. Hunter stepped into the office. A line was painted on the floor, just out of reach of the desk. The Chief Officer barked an instruction.

"Toe the line and stand to attention! Give your full name and number to the Governor!"

Hunter resisted the impulse to grin, staring hard at the clock above the Governor's head.

"One-three-three-seven. Hamish Hunter."

The Governor turned a page in a small file. "You're sentenced to two weeks' imprisonment without the option of a fine. Any questions?"

"I'm expecting a visitor," Hunter answered. "I read the regulations. This is an emergency. What do I do?"

The Governor took a good look at Hunter as if recalling something. The Chief Officer motioned Hunter outside. There was just time to hear ". . . at six o'clock last night, sir. The Deputy Governor saw her." Hunter waited a couple

160

of minutes before being recalled. The Governor's expression disclosed nothing. "I see you pleaded guilty. You've had ample time to put your affairs in order. I can't vary the rules without good reason. What *is* your reason?"

Hunter licked his lips. Both men were watching him closely. He did his best to sound convincing.

"It's a business matter. I'm a journalist. My office needs some notes that are in the possession of my fiancée. It's essential that they're delivered today."

The Governor's voice was uncompromising. "Not good enough. You're allowed a reception letter. Use it to tell this person whatever you want."

Hunter walked out without answering. It didn't end quite like that, they'd find out. Wanda might have to take a shotgun to someone but she'd get in. He climbed the iron staircase to the third floor. He filled a bucket with cold water and strapped on a pair of kneepads. For the next two hours, he scrubbed his way backwards round the gallery. Down below, a prison barber was assaulting the queer's hair style with clippers and scissors. A warder supervised the performance. A half-hour's exercise came at noon, taken on circular walks between cabbage patches. He walked alone, avoiding the overtures of the other men exercising.

Lunch was a metal container with potatoes, a strip of fat meat floating in tepid gravy. The afternoon chore was buffing the brass rail round the landing with a leather strop. The light was fading when someone shouted up from beneath.

"D/3 cleaner?"

It was a moment before Hunter realized that the summons was for him. He yelled back an answer. The jailer's call drifted up.

"Put your jacket and tie on and come down here."

He combed his hair hurriedly and ran downstairs. His escort took him through a succession of doors, emerging in front of the Main Gates. Callers were being let in through the courtyard. On the other side of the bars, remand prisoners were going into the Visiting Boxes. The jailer shoved him into the Administration Building and rapped on a door bearing the emblem DEPUTY GOVERNOR. A man of Hunter's own age was sitting at a desk.

"Hunter? Do you know someone called Countess Yampolska?" He managed to make the question sound ridiculous.

"I do. She's my fiancée."

The Deputy Governor's face registered amazement. "Well, she's here to see you. You'll be allowed fifteen minutes. No discussion of prison matters."

The warder took him to a single-story structure. A sign said SOLICITORS' ROOMS. The hack unlocked a door, handing Hunter over to his colleague inside. Plain glass partitions divided the rooms. The jailer ushered him into the first. Wanda came to her feet, looking uncertainly at the warder as Hunter took her in his arms. He wasted no time, whispering hurriedly, his mouth deep in the hair over her ear.

"Film in the cottage. Letter and key in the mailbox."

He let her go, searching her eyes. She sat down, facing him. The jailer pulled a chair to the end of the table. She wore her military-style overcoat, striped shirt and tan corduroy skirt underneath. She kept her hands on the table, smiling at him.

"I had your message. I understood everything."

Hunter relaxed. "I was beginning to think they wouldn't let you see me. How'd you get in?"

She moved her shoulders elegantly. "I came last night.

They told me I wasn't allowed to see you. I went to the Home Office this morning. Mr. Benstead went with me. He's been so kind, Hamish."

Caution flooded Hunter's mind. "You do realize that this is a very private matter. The copy has to go straight to the office. I don't want anyone to see it, least of all Benstead."

Her dark blue eyes were untroubled. "Nobody will. I shall deliver it myself."

He cleared his throat. "There's another thing, darling. It's an explosive article. A lot of people are interested in it. They might bother you."

She was twisting the amethyst ring on her finger. "I've already noticed. Don't worry. I'm quite capable of taking care of myself." She smiled at the warder.

Hunter hesitated. "It's getting pretty late. It'll be the best part of three hours before you can get to the office. Did you arrange to see Mr. Rainham?"

She nodded easily. "I have an appointment with him first thing in the morning. Everything's under control, darling. I thought I'd spend the night at my aunt's in the country. Go to the office straight from there."

The hack was doodling on the visiting-order. Small squares inside circles. His expression was a mixture of alertness and boredom.

Hunter spoke rapidly. "Did Benstead say anything about the appeal?"

She frowned slightly. "Yes. He saw a barrister last night. The opinion is that your appeal wouldn't succeed under the circumstances. In fact he said your sentence might even be increased."

His shoulders rose and fell. "Ah well, I'll survive. It'll be a rest cure. I'm neither smoking nor drinking. You're sure you've got everything straight in your head — where to go, what to do?"

She met his look levelly. "Positive. I'll send you a message the moment the information's been delivered." She turned to the jailer. "Is he allowed a telegram?"

The hack suspended his doodling. "They'll read it to him."

Hunter stood up. "Then that's that. You'd better run, sweetheart."

The warder glanced at his watch. "You've still got five minutes."

"We don't need them," said Hunter. He held her close again, savoring the scent of her body. This time he kissed her mouth. "I love you," he added steadily.

She touched his mouth with her fingers. "Me too. And don't worry. I'll take care of everything."

The jailer touched a bell. They waited in the doorway as she wobbled across the cobbles on high heels. The gate-keeper let her into the courtyard and unlocked a wicket in the massive outside doors. There was a glimpse of the street — the red of the parked Mini. She turned round, waved and was gone.

Wanda Yampolska

23 February 1967

SHE SAT in the car, making up her face in the driving mirror. Of course it was the cottage — it had to be. She'd been a fool not to guess. Hunter must have mailed the film to himself the night he came back from Warsaw. She put the Mini in gear, driving confidently as if the large black Rover behind had no connection with her. She'd needed no warning from anyone to know that she was being watched. It was ironical. They were following her because she was Hunter's girl friend and for no other reason. They'd picked her up yesterday morning as she left the *Quest* building. Two men looking like salesmen. They'd trailed her faithfully, sometimes a pair, sometimes separate, making her meeting with Benstead almost impossible. As it was, she'd arrived at Westminster Pier an hour late, having lost her shadowers finally in the National Gallery. Benstead and she had ridden the small pleasure steamer to Greenwich and back. He'd talked and she'd listened. Hunter's imprisonment seemed to have shaken Benstead. Time was running out, he insisted. It was at his urging that she had gone to the Home Office.

The Rover was still behind as she turned up Beaufort Gardens, heading for home. She glanced up at the driving mirror, just in time to see the passenger duck below the windshield. Instinct told her that he was using a radiophone. She parked, collected some cleaning on the corner and walked round to Bell Street. She ran up the steps and turned her key. Her father was out. She packed a case with clothes and put her passport in her handbag. Above all she had to be mobile. She added her mother's picture to the things she was taking and looked round the room. She could walk out of here, the house, England, without a tug of regret for a dying way of living. Benstead had promised that she'd be in Poland before Hunter's release. The thought was exhilarating.

She let herself out to the street again. The Rover was parked facing the corner, its lights out. She left her case in her car and walked to the phone booths by the Forum Cinema. One of the men shadowing her followed. He halted, twenty yards away, looking in a shop window. She dialed, keeping her eyes on him. Benstead answered. She gave him the news with a sense of triumph. His approval was cautious. Say nothing more on the phone — meet him as soon as she could. She hung up, looking through the glass. Her pursuer was still at his post. Benstead's final warning was superfluous. Her plan was the essence of simplicity.

She walked back to her car and drove up Gunter's Grove. She stopped in front of a walled building. A white board in the small front garden said: ST. ANSELM'S CONVENT SCHOOL (*Day-Girls and Boarders*). She carried her bag up the steps and rang the bell. The Rover had parked a few houses away, under the trees. The driver extinguished his lights again. Her smile was fleeting. It was just as well — he was going to have a long wait. A tiny nun answered the door, her face a white dot in a black hood. She pulled Wanda into the dim hall. Her hands fluttered in delight.

"Glory be to God, Wanda! What on earth — here, let me take your bag."

The smells, sights and sounds took her back years. Nothing had changed. There were the same waxed floors and reek of incense. The life-size Christ still hung with his crown of thorns. His Mother beside him with fresh daffodils at her feet. Near the door was the beaded figure of St. Anselm. A boarder was practicing scales in the music room down the corridor.

The tiny nun covered her mouth with her hand, shaking her head at her own excitement. Wanda spoke quickly.

"Do you think Reverend Mother could see me, Sister Philomena?"

The nun nodded. She led the way, weighed down by Wanda's bag. She paused in a doorway and fluttered her fingers shyly.

"I'll fetch her now, good-bye, dear."

The waiting room was hung with pictures of hockey teams and tennis matches, batches of first communicants. Her own face stared back from a group of fourteen-year-olds on their way to Lourdes. It seemed a long time since she had learned that miracles belonged to men and not to God. She sat down in a high-backed chair, feet crossed at the ankles. She rose, kissing the hand of the woman who came in. The nun hugged her warmly.

"God save us, child!" The French accent was still discernible. "What a wonderful surprise for me. Let me have a look at you!" She tugged Wanda into the light, her movements elegant in spite of the clumsy shoes and robes. Her middle-

167

aged features had an austere handsomeness. Calm eyes searched Wanda's face.

"What is it, my child?"

Wanda blinked back tears. "I'm in trouble, Reverend Mother. A man. He's started annoying me, following me to work — telephoning me at home. He's making my life impossible."

The older woman frowned. "But what does he want, dear?"

Wanda looked away. "He's made that obvious. And he's a married man."

A hint of toughness crept into the other woman's voice. "Is he, indeed. Well, we'll see about that. Don't worry, dear. There's a detective-inspector at Chelsea police station — they know how to deal with rascals like this."

Wanda shook her head vehemently. "I can't go to the police, Reverend Mother. My father would never forgive me. This man's a friend of his. I'll *have* to tell my father sooner or later but I'm afraid. The man's outside now."

The nun glided to the window and peered through a chink in the blind.

"There's a black car — is that him?"

Wanda nodded assent. "I've taken two weeks off from work. I thought it might help."

"You can stay here," the nun said readily. "If he bothers you then he'll find he has *me* to deal with — and that might not be so pleasant for him."

Wanda used her handkerchief on her eyes. "Everything's been arranged, Reverend Mother. I'm staying with friends in the country. I'll have to tell my father when I come home. What I wanted you to do was let me out the back way."

The answer was unhesitating. "Of course I will, dear." She took Wanda's hand in hers, collecting a key from a board as they went down the corridor. The chapel doors were open. Nuns and boarders knelt at Benediction. The Mother Superior crossed herself as she passed. She led the way across hard courts into the shadow of elms fringing a lawn. She unlocked a small door in the wall and withdrew the bolts. She pulled a face as the door creaked open. Her eyes were very bright as if the maneuver were part of some desperate adventure. She peered outside then kissed Wanda on both cheeks.

"There's nobody there! Now God bless you, and come and see me as soon as you're home. I want to know what happens."

The door opened on a street that was a hundred and fifty yards from the convent entrance. She hurried up to Old Brompton Road. A taxi was paying off in front of Coleherne Court. She caught the hack's eye.

"Grosvenor House Hotel."

She glanced back through the window as the cab accelerated. There was no sign of the Rover or its occupants. It was gone six when she walked into the hotel lobby. She turned left into the powder room, still carrying her bag. She locked herself in, changing into black stretch-pants, a sweater and flat shoes. She covered these with the short blue reefer coat. She left the hotel by the Park Lane entrance, hair tied in a scarf and wearing dark glasses. A cruising cab took her to Earl's Court. She left it opposite the station and hastened down the short street. There were no customers in the delicatessen store. The fat Pole jerked his head behind the counter. She opened the door and put her bag on the

169

floor. It was strange seeing Benstead here instead of Adam. Stranger even to find herself bound up dangerously with a man who, four days ago, she hadn't known existed. He was wearing the same shabby clothes and hat. His caped ulster was thrown across a tea-chest.

He sat with his hands on his knees, inspecting her attire thoroughly.

"You're certain you weren't followed?"

She lit a cigarette, giving an account of her exit from the convent. He nodded slowly, looking at her suitcase.

She flicked ash nervously. "I told you what Hamish said. He posted the film to himself in the country."

"You haven't told me *where* in the country."

"East Sussex — a village called Beckley. He rents a cottage. I'll sleep there. I'll be too late to catch a train back." She waited for his approval.

He cracked a mint pastille, wiping the fragments of white powder from his lips.

"Who else knows about this cottage? What about the people where he lives — his secretary?"

Her answer was definite. "He never spoke about it to anyone. I've only been there twice. He preferred to go there alone."

"Is there a phone?"

She thought for a moment. "Yes."

"Then keep away from it," Benstead said quickly. "I'll expect you at noon tomorrow — not here — we can't risk using the same meetingplace twice. Do you know the Tate Gallery?"

She nodded. "On the Embankment."

"Then twelve noon, just inside the entrance. Have the film

in a book. There are benches there. Sit down next to me then get up leaving the book behind. Neither of us speaks. Is that quite clear?"

"Quite clear," she said mechanically. "Have you heard any more from Warsaw — about me, I mean?"

He smiled, showing his large brown teeth. "I wasn't going to tell you till later. You leave on Monday. Take your passport to the Chancellery tomorrow for your visa. You realize it's likely that you'll never be able to return to this country?"

She looked at her watch. "I never want to. I'll have to go, otherwise I'll miss my train. Good night."

He stood up, craning down at her like some benevolent bird. "Good night, Wanda. Twelve noon tomorrow."

Stanley Dangerfield Benstead

23 February 1967

HE GLANCED round the room. Everything looked normal. The bed was ready for occupation, a book and a glass of water on the table beside it. Through the open kitchen door, the breakfast things stood ready. He unlocked the cabinet and pushed the 9-mm Parabellum inside his ulster. Its weight sagged in the deep pocket. He cut the lights and stepped into the hall. He waited for a minute before calling up the stairs. A door banged on the second-story landing.

"I'm going out again, Mrs. Riley. I might be a little late. Don't put the bolts on. I'll take care of everything when I come back."

The woman leaned over the banisters, looking down at him. The curlers had left her hair looking like a Hottentot's.

"Make sure you don't forget, then. Where are you going, Mr. Benstead, somewhere exciting, I'll bet. You never ask me to come," she finished coquettishly.

He shook his head. "I'm afraid it wouldn't be your idea of fun, Mrs. Riley. I'm playing chess with a friend."

"Well don't cheat," she said pertly.

He gave her the smile she expected and opened the street

door. He walked along the school wall and cut through to the subway station. He changed trains three times, emerging at Wapping. He made his way south, past cheap men's outfitters and ships' chandlers. Blocks of council flats and children's playgrounds marked the sites of wartime bomb damage. Cars were parked in front of pubs loud with the music of beat groups, the shrieking of transvestite talent shows. Over the last five years, dockside taverns had outstripped West End haunts in production of camp entertainment.

The wind blew wet in his face, carrying a hint of salt from the estuary. He turned left onto a causeway. Giant cranes reached above silent warehouses. Behind them shone the riding lights of half a dozen tramp steamers. He crossed the cobbled road to the dock gates. A Port of London Authority policeman was sitting in the hut by the entrance. He looked up from his newspaper. Benstead produced a pass. The cop scribbled something in a book.

"How long you going to be?"

Benstead moved his shoulders. "Half an hour or so. Not long, anyway."

The cop nodded. "OK. She's lying at Pier 4. Past that first crane. You can't miss her. You'll smell the sausage." He went back to his newspaper.

Bright arcs flooded the quayside, patterning the walls of the warehouses with twisted shapes of machinery. Benstead followed the single line trolley track. Donkey-engines clattered aboard the berthed ships. Bilge water spouted from their sides. A line of washing was ghostly on a darkened deck. He skirted the legs of the crane straddling the wharf. A gangplank creaked on his right, lifting and falling with the movement of the freighter. The ten-thousand tonner was new. A Polish pennant, limp with humidity, hung aloft under a courtesy flag. He walked up the gangplank to the boat deck. A man moved out of the shadows. Hatless, wearing a lettered jersey. Benstead addressed him in Polish. The seaman signaled him through a hatch. They climbed down a short ladder. Brightly colored tubes covered the ceiling of the corridor. The floor vibrated in sympathy with the engine room below. The seaman rapped on a door. He motioned Benstead inside and left.

The captain's cabin was roomy. A large bunk, a carpet, a row of books and a telephone. There was a picture of a woman with hair in a bun holding a baby, by the bunk. The captain heaved himself up from his table. Both portholes were open but the cabin was hot. He wore a cotton T-shirt and a pair of faded slacks. They shook hands. The captain rinsed a couple of glasses in a basin and poured from a bottle of vodka.

"*Zdrowie!*"

They clinked glasses and drank, standing. The captain was middle-aged with a broad face tapering to a spade of black beard. He closed both portholes and the door. Benstead unfastened his ulster.

"You have received confirmation of my instructions?"

The captain's smile showed more gold than enamel. "An hour ago. We leave on the first tide in the morning. The authorities have been informed. The pilot comes aboard at six."

Benstead shook a fresh pack of pastilles into his snuffbox. "And the rest?" He shook his head as the other offered the vodka bottle.

The captain pulled the door and led the way along the corridor. Down a gangway to a lower deck. The radio cabin was open. Benstead shut the door behind them. He sat down, putting on the headset — earphones and mouthpiece. He touched a switch and turned a control knob with delicate fingers. A needle moved on a dial, nudging into the fifteen-meter band. Sound roared in his ears, fading as he turned the tuning device. He still spoke in Polish.

"PLB Seven, calling Station WOB. PLB Seven, calling Station WOB. Are you receiving me. Over." He went on calling at intervals of ten seconds. It was even hotter here than above. Sweat had started to trickle from his armpits.

A voice was suddenly loud in the headphones. "Station WOB calling PLB Seven. I am receiving you clearly. Over."

Benstead licked the crust from dried lips. "PLB Seven for Central. Message follows. Goods loaded. Details tomorrow. Will you repeat the message? Over."

The reply was loud. "Goods loaded. Details tomorrow. Over."

"Correct, WOB. Over and out."

He took off the headset and thumbed down the switch. The captain was leaning against the wall, fanning himself with his hand.

"My cabin?" said Benstead.

The captain opened the door and jerked his head across the corridor. His golden smile was huge.

"You will find everything you asked for. The developing materials are in your locker."

Benstead stepped into the cabin. There were shoes, a cap and a merchant-navy uniform lying on the bunk. On top of the jacket were seaman's papers. His own picture was affixed to the top page of the booklet. Scribbled underneath was a name in his own handwriting. *Jerzy Rudzki.*

"The men?" he asked quickly.

The captain scratched the mat of black hair above his T-shirt. "In the tavern. They have been told to obey your instructions."

Benstead nodded. Nothing had been forgotten. "Then good night, captain." The door shut and he was alone. He dressed quickly, putting the uniform under his tweed suit. He changed shoes and put the seaman's papers in an inside pocket. The heavy automatic was still in his ulster. The caped garment hid any sign of bulkiness. He climbed back on deck and made his way down the gangplank. He checked in at the guard-point. The cop looked up, yawning.

"Get yourself a drink of that vodka? Know how they make it — dynamite and old socks." He grinned at his own joke and lifted his newspaper.

Benstead walked away. The guard changed at midnight. Three men were booked out from the Polish vessel. Three men would return. He crossed the cobbled causeway. A ship's siren hooted in midstream as he turned into the pub. The large bar was full of seamen. Shirt-sleeved barmen worked feverishly, sliding pots of beer along the wet counter. He pushed his way through the crowd, ignoring the come-on signals from a brassy hooker at the bar. The men he wanted were standing by the fireplace. Three of them, dressed in Polish merchant-marine uniform. One of them wore the flashes of a radio operator on his sleeve. Benstead lowered his voice, speaking to him.

"You know where to go."

The man shoved his way to the door and out to the street. Benstead jerked his head at the others.

"You two stay here till closing time, then go to the Texas Club. You don't need anything to get in. Just pay the entrance fee. Wait for me there. I'll be back before three."

The shorter of the two had a scar from nose to mouth. It twisted as he answered.

"The machine is outside."

Benstead took the proffered key. The lavatories were on the street. He put a coin in the slot and pushed. He stripped off the top layer of clothing, bundling it with his hat inside the ulster. He walked slowly back towards the river, a seaman's cap on his bald head. He stopped at the retaining wall. Water slapped on the other side. There was no one in sight. He dropped the bundle into the river. It floated for a few seconds, drifted as a soggy mass and then vanished. He hurried back to the pub. A motorcycle was propped against the curb. He donned the helmet and windbreaker strapped on the pillion. Goggles covered most of his face. The weight of the gun was a solid reassurance against his belly. He turned the key, kicking the motor to life. Its staccato roar faded down the short length of street.

Benjamin du Sautoy-Smith

23 February 1967

HE CAME IN through the front way. The General's things were hanging on their hook in the cloakroom. The messenger took Smith's coat and umbrella.

"They're all in the Annex, sir."

Smith nodded. A quarter to six. He was nearly an hour late. There was a note on his desk. *God damn and blast it, Benjy!* A trail of ink spots spattered the paper where the pen had been slammed down with force. He grabbed a handful of cigarettes from a box and went out through the french windows. The sergeant was on his feet before Smith reached the Code Room. He snapped a salute and moved aside letting Smith pass. The cork-lined door clicked shut. The operator took off his headset.

"I'm glad you came, sir. I've been storing stuff for you for a couple of hours. I've got it on separate tapes. The Fulham number's been dead. But the G.P.O. monitored all the public phones within a radius of five hundred yards from the house. Sanderson called in at four fifty-seven. The subject had just gone into a telephone box. I've located it on the list. It's on the Fulham Road, near the Forum Cinema. It's the only call Sanderson identified. The rest's routine. Do you want to hear the call now, sir?"

Smith shook his head. The operator's eyes were curiously expectant.

"In a minute. Get me Sanderson."

He took the headset, holding the receiver away from his ear as the operator threw a switch. Music blared behind the answer.

"Turn that bloody thing off," he snapped. "I can't hear myself, let alone you." The car radio was silenced. He went on. "Right. Now where's your subject and where are you?"

The operator stilled the auxiliary generator. Sanderson's voice was suddenly loud.

"Gunter's Grove, sir. Between Fulham Road and The Boltons. It's a convent-school for girls — St. Anselm's. She went in at seventeen hours o-eight, alone. Her car's outside. A light came on in one of the front windows. It's still on. Did you get that bit about the prison?"

The operator pointed at one of the tapes. Smith ignored him. "*What* about the prison? I've just this minute come in."

"She visited Hunter at a quarter to four, left at ten past. We've been on her tail ever since. She made one telephone call from a box. I gave Robby the time."

Smith covered the mouthpiece with his hand. "Has the D.D. been down here?" The operator moved his head from side to side. Smith spoke to Sanderson again. "Have you checked the place for a back door? *A back door, man!* You can't tell which gardens belong *where*? Well, look! Climb a wall if you have to. I'll call you back in twenty minutes."

He cradled the headset, looking at the operator. "All right,

179

let's hear the tape." He shut his eyes, listening intently as the spool started revolving. A phone bell rang. There was the click of a receiver being lifted. The woman's voice was triumphant. *I've just left him. I know where the film is.* A cautious voice answered. Smith stiffened with recognition. He opened his eyes, fumbling for a cigarette. He stared at the match, listening incredulously as answer followed question. He heard the tape to the end, the two voices implanting their message in his mind. It was some time before he realized that the spool now turned soundlessly. The operator was doing his best to appear as if he had not understood. Smith came to his feet slowly. "You'll keep your mouth shut about this, Sergeant. Get the duty-officer to order a Q. car. Have the tapes and that machine put in it. And I want Captain Pinner. Tell him to wait for me in my room."

He nodded at the man waiting outside without seeing him and went up the stairs. The top floor of the house had been gutted. Three rooms were thrown into one. A large-scale map of Berlin was unrolled on a wall. A powerful lamp illuminated it. He came into the room with the cigarette in his lips still unlit. The General was sitting at the head of the table. Smith recognized the two men with him. Moncrieff from Berlin and the liaison man from the Home Office. He sat down slowly, conscious that all three were watching him curiously. He took his time with a match, avoiding the General's eye. The General's silver watch was lying face-up on the table. He put it back in his waistcoat pocket.

"Well, Benjy?" he asked expectantly.

He heard his own voice, the stilted formal tone of a lawyer bringing news of a disaster.

"May I have a word with you in private, sir?"

The General's grizzled eyebrows lifted fractionally. He glanced at the other two and then rose.

"You'll excuse us?"

Smith followed him outside. They stood at the top of the staircase, facing one another. The voices inside the Conference Room were no more than a dull murmur. A picture of the Duke of Wellington mounted on a white charger hung against the paneling. The Director squared the frame to his liking before speaking impatiently.

"Well, come on, Benjy — what is it?"

Smith cleared his throat. "I didn't want to say it in there, sir. I've just established that Benstead is a plant. He's working for the Poles."

The General's eyes were instantly alert. "Are you sure?"

Smith moved his head. "I'm afraid so, sir. You'll hear for yourself. The thing is, he's one short step away from what we need. I don't know how much more damage has been done. But he *has* been positively vetted. Under the circumstances I'll expect you to approve my resignation when . . ."

The General cut in brusquely. "Come off it, Benjy, for God's sake! What do you mean, 'one short step away'?"

Smith explained. "The woman got in to see Hunter this afternoon. He's told her where the film is. Now she's delivering it to Benstead."

"And where is she?" the General asked quickly.

Smith took a deep breath. "In a convent in Fulham, with any luck. But I doubt it. It doesn't really matter, sir. Hunter's going to tell us where she is. This time he'll talk. That at least I'm sure about."

181

The General dragged his watch out. "All right, Benjy. Let's get this thing over as quickly as we can. And don't let the buggers catch on that anything's wrong. Try to look as if you know what you're up to." He opened the door, his arm wrapped easily about Smith's shoulders.

He sat down, motioning at the man from the Home Office. "Mr. Wright?"

The young man had pale smooth wings of hair over his ears. His manner was like his clothes, elegantly casual.

"The Minister instructs me to make his position absolutely clear, sir. We have no official knowledge of Malek other than as a naturalized British Subject. As far as we're concerned, he's in good standing. If and when you make application for political asylum for the other two people, it would be granted on the understanding that the privilege would be strictly temporary and entirely your responsibility. I think that's about it, sir."

The General touched a bell. "Thank you, Mr. Wright. Tell the Minister that he'll have a letter from the Director at the appropriate time. They'll show you out downstairs."

He grunted as the door closed and lit his pipe. "Make it as brief as you can. You've got three people to pick up on Sunday. How are you going to do it?"

Moncrieff rose and went to the wall, a short man with a crumpled face and dark darting eyes. He drew a circle on the map with a pointer. His voice had the certainty of someone used to exposition.

"We've acted on the assumption that Malek will turn up somewhere within this circle. He's crossed the Havel near Spandau half a dozen times in the past and he's an exponent

182

of the double-bluff. Nevertheless, things have changed since his day. There's a heavy water patrol, fast boats equipped with sonar equipment. We know that the Russians put down an antisubmarine net. Their missile posts are radar-controlled. They've got enough conventional firepower in the watchtowers in between to knock anything larger than a sparrow out of the sky. I understand someone over here suggested a helicopter going in low over the water, under their radar screen. I'd give that idea three minutes after crossing the line. The noise alone would finish it. What we've done is this. We've had a man in Potsdam since yesterday. He'll collect Malek and bring him to the Berlin-Wannsee frontier. We've had a couple of Vopos there on ice for some weeks, ready to defect. They'll come with Malek and the others. All we need now is the time and place to contact him."

The General knocked his pipe out noisily, his voice loud and confident.

"You'll have that tomorrow — when would you say, Benjy, some time in the morning?"

Smith turned his head. Imagination had provided a tall man in an ulster crossing the room, shoulders stooped and looking like a large awkward bird.

"Tomorrow morning," he agreed.

Moncrieff returned his things to his briefcase. His movements were swift and positive. He glanced from Smith to the General.

"Just one last thing, sir. We've been getting our own signals in Berlin. Warsaw's tighter than a drum at the moment. They seem to know two things for sure — Malek's on the loose and D-day is Sunday. They've been picking people up for the last forty-eight hours. Malek's about as hot as he could be. Whoever comes with him is a hazard. This is my personal opinion, of course."

Shreds of tobacco were still burning in the General's ashtray. He ground them out with the bowl of his pipe.

"Three is the number. I don't want *any* of them lost."

Moncrieff fastened the belt of his raincoat. "Fair enough, sir. You know where I am if you want me. I'll stay in the hotel till I hear from you." He looked round, tapping his pockets as if to make sure he had left nothing behind.

They waited till the door closed. The General's tiptoe walk took him to the wall and back. He stopped in front of Smith, his leathery fingers pointing.

"It had to come, damn it, Benjy. You're no more infallible than I am."

Smith took his hands out of his pockets. "The chess player! I want you to promise me one thing, sir. When we get Benstead, I want half an hour alone with him. No, it's not what you think — I just want to talk to him. He won't break but at least I'll learn something about myself."

The General's tone was dry. "There's something you have to learn about Hunter first. I'm coming to the prison with you. You don't mind?"

Smith's chair scraped back. "I'm not in a position to mind, sir. I take it I'm still in charge?"

The General threw the door wide. "Get off your high horse, you're in no position for that either. Make your arrangements with Pinner and give me a shout when you're ready to move."

They walked down the stairs, aware of each other's concern and strengthened by it. Smith stopped at the Code Room.

184

The tape recorder had already gone. The operator motioned with his head.

"Everything's in the car, sir."

Smith held out his hand for the phone. "Get me Sanderson again." He spoke standing up. "What's happening?"

Sanderson's voice was uncertain. "The light's gone out in the front room. Her car's still here."

Smith was sure of the reply before he spoke. "You checked the place for a back door?"

"Yes, sir. There is one — behind some tennis courts. But it doesn't look as if it's been opened in months."

But it *had* been opened, thought Smith. Yampolska had walked out, leaving them to watch her car for her. Minutes could count now. He spoke, keeping his anxiety to himself.

"Stay where you are. If she shows up, grab her."

He made his way through the door connecting the two gardens. He could see Pinner beyond the trees, waiting in his room. He ran up the steps and shut the french windows. The man inside had short hair and a nose like a scythe blade. He was holding a pad and pencil at the ready. Smith wasted no time.

"Get onto the Special Branch — Commander Collins. Tell him this is top priority. I want a stop put on all ports — the full treatment. He's looking for a man and a woman. Stanley Dangerfield Benstead and Countess Wanda Yampolska. *Records* will supply photographs. It's probable the man is armed. If they get them together, they're to be kept apart. Is that clear?"

Pinner scribbled the names on his pad. "They'll want a holding charge, sir. They always do."

Smith paused, the drawer half open. "The Defense of the

Realm Act. If they don't like that, tell them to choose their own."

Pinner had gone before Smith had the gun from the drawer. The weapon had a two-inch barrel, thirty-eight caliber. He pushed it into his left breast pocket and picked up the green phone.

"Get me West Wellow — the College. I want to speak to Colonel Titmus."

He waited for his connection, staring through the french windows into the darkness. His fingers drummed nervously on the desk. Once they started moving, he'd be better. The line came alive. He spoke rapidly.

"George? Benjy. Don't ask questions, just listen. I want three of your best instructors — unarmed combat, that sort of thing. Give them one of the jeeps with civilian markings. They're to dress in track suits — the gear they wear on duty — and be outside Brixton Prison in an hour's time. That's right, Brixton Prison. *Yes,* you'll get them back, George. And thanks."

He hung up and spoke into the intercom box. "I'm ready when you are, sir."

He had his things on before the General appeared in the hall. A three-liter Rover was parked outside. The wind had dropped, leaving the air cold and damp. A couple of lights still burned in the publisher's offices opposite. Otherwise the street was in darkness. He climbed in behind the wheel. The tape recorder was on the back seat. The General sat beside him, bowler hat in his lap, watching as Smith tested the controls. A radiophone was hooked under the dash. The General stretched his legs as far as they would go and settled back.

"Like old times, Benjy. I told my wife I wouldn't be in for dinner."

A quarter to seven. Smith swung the car into the Whitehall traffic. The steering was light and direct. The heavy chassis would hold round bends at a hundred miles an hour without drifting.

"That's one problem at least I don't have," he said briefly.

"Perhaps it's just as well." The General glanced through the window, shrewd eyes missing nothing. "I don't know what you have in mind for Hunter, Benjy. But I've been on to the Home Office. We can have him if we want him. The Governor is expecting us."

Smith forked right and then left behind Millbank. The Embankment would give him a clear run as far as Battersea. Hunter had occupied part of his brain for three days — the test of strength between them almost an obsession. He'd won — but the knowledge left him strangely dissatisfied, as if something between them were still unfinished. Hunter had lost in the dirtiest way of all — betrayed by a woman he loved. And it was left to an enemy to tell him so.

Smith shifted a hand from the wheel to grope for a cigarette. "I want him out," he said truthfully. "We owe him that at least. He's got a jolt coming to him."

The General held a match to Smith's cigarette. "You're getting almost human, Benjy. I wonder why that is?"

Smith turned his head quickly. The General's eyes were innocent. They made fast time through Clapham, hitting Brixton Hill halfway up the long drag to Streatham. He turned down the lane to the jail. No cars were outside. He cut his lights and used the phone. He replaced it, shrugging.

"They're still in front of the convent. They've got a long wait ahead."

He lifted the tape recorder from the rear seat. The General rang the bell, a spare figure in his bowler hat. He lowered his voice as keys jangled in the courtyard.

"Behave yourself, Benjy. We don't want to spend the night here."

The postern gate opened. Iron gates faced them. Beyond that the grim silhouettes of the cellblocks. Smith gave the warder a name. The man's eyes were respectful.

"The Governor's waiting for you, sir. Will you come this way, please?" He opened a second postern in the iron gates. He pointed his keys ahead. "The door straight in front of you."

Lights burned in the Reception Wing. There was a glimpse of movement behind barred windows as they crossed the stretch of tarmac. A door opened in the Administration Building. A man came to the head of the steps, peering from one to the other.

"My name's Hawker. I'm the Governor."

The General lifted his hat. They followed the Governor into his office. A fire burned in the grate. There were some bad pictures, a desk and chairs. On top of the desk was a model of a sailing ship built from matchsticks. Smith put the tape machine on the floor. There was a power socket in the wainscoting near the fireplace. The General glanced round incuriously.

"You know why we're here, Governor. We'd like to see Hunter alone if that's possible."

The Governor nodded. "I'll have him brought from his

cell. He hasn't been told anything. My instructions are that he'll be leaving with you. The Home Office has ordered a Special Release. His clothes and property will have to be made ready."

Smith looked up. "There's another car arriving. If they ask at the gate, will you see they're told to wait?"

They watched the Governor cross the tarmac to the Reception Wing. Smith bent down, plugging the machine into the wall socket. He found the General's eyes fastened on him.

"It'll be all yours," the General said quietly. "I'll do my best to keep my mouth shut."

They waited in silence. Half an hour went by. Suddenly a gate banged. The noise echoed in the corridors of the Reception Block. Smith went to the window. The Governor was crossing the yard, Hunter beside him. The Canadian's hand chopped the air as if making a point. Whatever he said had its effect. The Governor's face was red when they came into the office. He summoned what was left of his dignity.

"I'll leave it to you to explain the purpose of this interview. Hunter's concerned about it."

The Canadian looked from the General to Smith. "Nobody has to explain anything. I recognize one of my oldest and dearest friends."

He dropped into a chair as the door closed behind the Governor. Two days in jail had left their mark. His face seemed thinner, the lines deeper from nose to mouth. His eyes looked as if they had been open too long without rest. They fixed on Smith, the dislike in them implacable. He smoothed toffee-gray hair.

"What the hell do *you* want?" he asked bluntly.

Smith accepted the challenge. "You were visited this afternoon by Countess Yampolska. What you refused to tell me, you told her."

Hunter dragged his chair forward a little, as if to take better stock of Smith. His clothes showed signs of a hasty pressing. He took the cigarette the General offered, nodding thanks without even glancing at the older man. His eyes were always on Smith.

"Countess Yampolska visited me," he said warily. "And we talked about business matters. Don't you approve of the idea?"

Smith held out a match. Hunter leaned into the flame. Firelight touched the back of his neck. Right where the axe would take him, thought Smith. The sooner it was lowered, the better for everyone.

"You told her where the film was," he said steadily. "And I'll tell you what else you did. You handed the lives of your friend's children to the Communists."

Hunter's grin showed his front teeth. "I've heard it all a million times. Look, if this release is something to do with you and there are strings tied to it, I can always go back to my cell."

The General's hands were clasped. He was studying the floor at his feet. Smith went on.

"You said you were resilient the other night. I hope it's true, for your own sake. We're going to listen to a recording of a telephone conversation. The caller used a public phone not far from Bell Street. The time, late this afternoon."

He touched the switch on the tape machine. The General

190

was still looking at the floor. Hunter's grin widened as the spool started unwinding. It faded with the sound of a woman's voice, cool yet triumphant.

"I've just left him. He's told me where the film is."

Caution was in the answer. *"Where are you talking from? Wherever it is, they won't be far away. You realize this?"*

Yampolska. *"I'm in a box, quite a way from the house. They followed me in a car from the prison. Two of them. One's standing about thirty yards away. I can see him through the mirror as I'm talking."*

Benstead. *"How are you going to get rid of them?"*

Yampolska. *"That's already taken care of — don't worry about it."*

Benstead. *"Good, then listen. Don't use this number any more. Things are happening. It might be tapped at any moment. I can't even be sure of my own position any more. It's vital that we get the information to Warsaw as soon as possible."*

A short pause. Yampolska. *"It'll take me some time. It's seventy miles. I mean where I have to go. Can we wait till the morning?"*

Benstead. *"Yes. No more now. Meet me in the delicatessen as soon as you can. And be doubly careful."*

The loose end of the tape whipped round the spool. Smith switched off the machine. Hunter's face was completely without color. The tic was jumping under his eye. He spoke with an air of bewilderment — like a man who turns his head to find a stranger standing where a friend stood.

"That's Benstead."

Smith pulled the plug from the socket, watching Hunter cautiously.

"They're Communist agents, both of them. As long as the film stays in her possession, we've still got a chance. Where is it?"

The Canadian looked at the General again. Shock dulled his voice. "Down at the cottage. A cottage I rent. We were going to be married — do you realize that?"

Smith turned his hand over slowly. The gesture apologized for something undefined — the woman's treachery — his own ruthless persistence.

"I'm sorry. Did Benstead know about the cottage?"

Hunter wiped his mouth on the back of his hand. The attempt at a smile failed.

"Funny — this is one time I could really use a drink. No, Benstead doesn't know. She's only been there a couple of times. I had to tell her where the letter would be. The mailbox isn't in the house."

The General cleared his throat noisily. Smith turned, expecting a comment, but the General stayed silent. Smith continued.

"You hate my guts, Hunter." He tapped the top of the tape machine. "Doing this to you hasn't exactly improved the situation. But lives are at stake — will you help?"

Hunter's face had regained its color. But bitterness showed in the set of his mouth.

"I'll tell you what you've done. You've opened my eyes to every dirty dodge and caper she's pulled over the years. And I can see myself. A middle-aged delinquent shuffling out to the sound of a large fat horselaugh. What do you expect me to be — grateful to you? Suppose I said this. Screw you. Screw Korwin. And screw you again. How would *that* sound to you?" His hands were shaking violently.

Smith lit another cigarette and passed it to him. Hunter was near breaking-point.

"You're free. You can walk out of here and go about your business. Nobody'll bother you any more. But three people will die. It's up to you."

Hunter shook his head as if ridding his brain of the image. "What'll happen to her?"

Smith shrugged. Hunter no longer used her name. "She'll be tried. They'll both be tried."

Hunter nodded. "I want to be there when the book's thrown at them. Can you understand that or is it too primitive, too vindictive, for your charitable soul?"

"I can understand it," Smith answered quietly.

Hunter got up and went to the window. He looked across the yard at the lighted cellblock. Suddenly he swung round.

"I won't *tell* you where the cottage is — but I'll show you. Are we in business?"

Smith nodded. The General came to his feet, moving with surprising agility.

"Then let's get out of here."

The Governor was waiting on the steps. The General nodded shortly.

"Thank you, Governor. Mr. Hunter's leaving with us."

The jailer let them through into the courtyard. The Governor accompanied them to the postern. A large slate hung on the wall outside the gatekeeper's lodge.

ROLL CALL

Remand   317
Convicted   102
At Court   11
          ────
           430

The warder erased the total, altering the figure to 429. He opened the small door to the street. Hunter and the General climbed into the Rover. Smith crossed to the parked jeep. The four men inside were dressed in dark track suits. All were hatless. Smith put his head through the open window.

"Who's in charge, here?"

The man sitting beside the driver snapped a salute. "I am, sir. Staff-Sergeant O'Connor."

"Then listen, Sergeant — this applies to all of you. You're going on a mission that might easily become lively. Our objective is to arrest two people — first a woman, then, with luck, a man. It's possible they might provide more opposition than we expect. Your orders are to use all the force you feel necessary. The main thing is to *get* the bastards. We're trying to stay clear of the police. What equipment have you brought with you?"

The sergeant had a narrow, intelligent face. "The Colonel issued small arms, sir. Webley forty-fives. There's an extendible ladder. Digging tools. A searchlight. We brought a P.G.L. box — the usual stuff — flares, camera, the electronic gear."

Smith moved his head. "Right. I'll keep down to sixty. Don't get too far behind. And you stop for nothing, do you

194

understand. If you hit anything, keep going. We'll worry about it afterwards. Everything clear?"

There was a murmur of assent. Smith walked back to the Rover. Hunter was in the back seat, his face icily remote. Smith turned behind the wheel.

"Do you still need that drink? We can make a quick stop somewhere."

It was said without offense but he read Hunter's level stare and was sorry. Sorry, he thought. A little more of this and he'd be apologizing.

"I need nothing," Hunter answered flatly.

Smith switched on the ignition. "What's our quickest way?"

"The Hastings Road," said Hunter. "Head for Camberwell. It's posted plainly from there."

Smith put his foot down. Rubber ground into grit as the car gathered speed. The two vehicles rolled the length of the prison wall, twenty yards apart under a damp ragged sky.

Wanda Yampolska

23 February 1967

THE SHORT TRAIN halted with a jolt. A voice somewhere at the back shouted out the name of the station. She threw the door open hurriedly and climbed down. A couple of lamps lit the deserted waiting room. A torn poster fluttered in the wind. She picked up her bag, watching the rear lights of the train disappear down the track into the darkness. A sack of mail had been dumped in front of the station exit. A uniformed figure appeared, pushing a trolley. The man stopped as he saw her.

"Can I have your ticket, please, miss?"

She put her case down, fumbling in her bag. "What are the fast trains back to London in the morning?"

He took her ticket. He had flat feet and a slow country voice.

"They'm running five minutes past the hour, seven till eleven, miss." He trundled his trolley away.

A G.P.O. van was parked outside, otherwise the station yard was empty. She started down the slope, walking easily in her slacks and low shoes. The mail-van overtook her, its head-lamps sweeping beyond the low hedges as it turned the bend. The way wound along the bottom of the valley. The week's heavy rain had left the fields on each side water-logged. The solid white line in the middle of the road was a guide for her. A quarter of a mile on, a signpost glimmered. She turned right onto a hardtopped lane sheltered by hawthorn and briar. Low threatening clouds scudded overhead on the wind. After another mile she saw the first lights of the village. There were no more than half a dozen buildings. A church and a vicarage. A general store with a gas pump. A couple of cottages. A pub with a few cars in front of it. The lane came to a dead end and a couple of hundred yards further on was blocked by the gates to an Elizabethan manor house. Laughter was loud in the pub. She avoided the lighted expanse in front. She was looking for a path on her right. A small white gate with a shingle located it. She pushed the gate open. A bell hanging on a spring tinkled. Walls enclosed a small, matted garden, split by a flagged pathway. The cottage stood at its end. The ugliness of the building was partially hidden by creeper clinging to sagging trelliswork. A small box on a post was just inside the gate. She put her bag on the ground and groped for the key under the weatherproof cover. She undid the padlock. There were four letters inside the mailbox, a second key. She struck a match. The top envelope was addressed in Hunter's handwriting. She tore the flap and felt the small square of celluloid inside. She hurried down the path and through the front door.

The room had a cellar-like stink of disuse. She pulled the curtains and switched on the lights. It was almost a year since she had been there. Nothing had changed. Leaves had blown down the chimney onto the shabby carpet, an incongruous souvenir of fall. There was a small-screen television set on a stand — odd chairs and table — a moth-eaten fox's brush and horseshoe on the wall. A picture of Hunter on a gray gelding stood on the mantelpiece. There were two bedrooms off the passage, one left, one right. Beyond them a kitchen and bathroom. She undid the back door. Another patch of unkempt garden sloped down to a hedge. A cart-track ran through the pastureland on the other side, up to the forest. The dense stand of oak and chestnut trees covered five hundred acres, protecting the manor house from the winter gales.

She shut the door again and went back to the sitting room. The rest of the mail was bills. She shook the minute squares of film onto the tablecloth. There were four of them, each smaller than the amethyst on her finger. She took off her reefer coat, shook her hair free and sat down. She lit a cigarette, staring at the pieces of film with growing excitement. On Monday she'd be in Poland. It was difficult to grasp the idea of a completely new life — new values. What mattered above everything else was that her work would be recognized and rewarded. What she would leave behind was no more than what she despised.

She got up, searching the bookshelves for Hunter's work-box. She found it under a pile of paperbacks. Spare type-writer ribbons, Chinese-ink pens, paper clips, a roll of cel-lotape. She picked a book at random, a cheap anthology of verse. She slid the four pieces of microfilm between the pages and sealed them with tape. She left the book on the table and opened up the right-hand bedroom. There were no sheets and blankets. It didn't matter. She'd sleep on the floor rather than use the bed she'd shared with Hunter.

There was no food in the kitchen. That didn't matter either. She wasn't hungry. There was tea and sugar, some canned milk and fruit. Enough for her breakfast. A quarter to ten. She carried the bag into the bedroom, turned off the lights and stretched out fully clothed.

The occasional noise drifted through the open window. Voices from the pub. Cars along the Hastings Road. The stutter of a motorcycle. She drowsed for a while, vaguely conscious of a dog's hysterical yapping. The faint tinkle of a bell brought her bolt upright on the bed. *The gate.* The wind, perhaps. She slipped from the bed to the window. Hollyhocks dead since last year rustled in the shadows. She moved very quietly to the back door and inched the bolts back. She left the door open, tiptoeing round the side of the house. She could see a faint blaze above the wall, in the direction of the pub. Suddenly she smelled it on the wind, the unmistakable crushed-mint smell that belonged to one man. She turned the corner.

Benstead was standing by the front door, head concealed in a motorcyclist's helmet, Perspex goggles hiding his eyes. He caught her arm before she could scream, hurrying her back into the house. He shut the door and stripped off helmet and goggles. He moved his neck as if it pained him.

"Have you got the film?"

She pointed dumbly into the sitting room. Her mouth was completely dry. She sat down suddenly, her legs no longer bearing her weight.

"God, you frightened me," she said with feeling.

The sparse gray hair lay limp on his bald head. He was wearing a cloth windbreaker over some sort of uniform trousers. The edges of his lips were crusted with flecks of white powder. He looked at her fully for a minute before he answered.

"Give me the film. There's been a change of plan."

The first shock had gone. His words provided a fresh source of anxiety. *She wasn't going to Poland on Monday.* She got up slowly and led the way into the sitting room. She showed him the book. He separated the pages and carried the film to the light. He replaced them, leaving the book on the table. His eyes were on the phone. She shook her head.

"I haven't touched it. What change of plan — is it something to do with me?"

He turned from the window slowly. She noticed that he was still wearing his gloves. Something in his eyes told her why. The bell jangled on the gate, breaking her sudden spell of terror. Steps sounded down the path outside. Benstead pushed her towards the door.

"Nothing's the matter. Whoever it is, get rid of them."

He whipped into Hunter's bedroom. Light from the passage shafted through the open door. It closed gently but not before she had seen the gun in Benstead's hand. A silencer was screwed onto the barrel.

Her mind jumped like a hunted animal's as someone thudded the door knocker. She dragged the door wide. A man in his late thirties was standing on the step, tweed-suited and ruddy. He lifted his hat, round face offering a pleasant smile.

"Good evening. I saw the lights from the pub. I'm Peter Powell. Is Hamish here?"

Eyes a little bloodshot looked past her curiously. The door of Hunter's bedroom was still closed. She took the man's sleeve, knowing that at all costs she had to get him into the house.

"No, he's not. But he'll be here tomorrow. I'm expecting him to phone any minute. Please do come in. Let me get you a drink."

He stepped in, smelling of scotch, and amiable. "You must be Wanda. I've heard a lot about you. I keep a few horses. Hamish hacks out with me." He nodded at the picture of the gray gelding.

She poured scotch into a tumbler, trying to stop her fingers from shaking. She put the glass by his elbow and picked up the book containing the film. All she had to do now was reach her bedroom. She pulled her hair behind her ears, looking full into his eyes.

"I won't be a minute," she promised. Ten steps along the passage. She did her best not to run. Hunter's room was still in darkness. She closed her own door and turned the key. Her hands flew as she threw her things into her bag. She crammed the book on top of the clothing and shut the bag. She grabbed her coat and went through the open window. The grass was slippery. The hedge caught at her hair, ripping the skin on the backs of her hands as she forced her way through. She stumbled up the cart-track, sliding in cow dung, her breathing painful. Her back felt naked. She closed her eyes on the memory of the gun, expecting to hear its cough behind her. She stopped on the edge of the wood. Nothing moved in front of her. There was a complete absence of sound. No wind stirred the bare branches of the trees. Just silence and shadow. A door banged at the bottom of the hill. The visitor appeared with Benstead as she watched. Both were talking animatedly. A couple of minutes later, a car started up. Then a motorcycle. The light of a single headlamp appeared at the bottom of the cart-track. She was just able to vanish into the trees as the light swept the place where she had been standing.

She left the rough track, running in as straight a line as she could. The ground sloped upwards. A carpet of rotting leaves covered it, into which her feet sank. She began to see better, her eyes adjusting to the obscurity. The stutter of the motorcycle behind stopped suddenly. The forest had the strange stillness that comes with winter dusk. It was too early yet for the nocturnal marauders to manifest themselves. She dropped down, burrowing into the ground as the brilliance of the one headlamp pierced the darkness. The dank leaves smelled bitter. Unnamed horrors crawled across her face. She lay perfectly still, the beam passing over her body.

Benstead was standing in the middle of the track, turning the handlebars of his machine so that the headlamp moved through an arc. He pushed on a few yards, searching the trees to his left. He wasted no time calling for her. Neither had she to see or hear him to know his objective. Cunning restrained her panic. If she could reach the road — or a house — a trumped-up story would provide transport. Somehow she had to get back to London. She had a wild idea of taking the first plane out, regardless of its destination. Paris, Zurich, Berlin. From there she could go to Warsaw, deliver the film with the story of Benstead's treachery. She accepted his intention to kill her, without understanding the motive. But the idea of a plane was hopeless. There was no time. The deadline was only a day and a half away. Her only chance was to go to the Embassy. Somebody there would know what to do with the film and give her protection.

The light was stationary now. Benstead had propped the machine, leaving the beam pointing in her direction. He was coming slowly through the trees towards her, the gun in his hand. She could hear his breathing, shallow and labored. If she stayed where she was, he would walk right over her. He was only yards away as she sprang to her feet. She could still outpace him, even running with the bag. She twisted away from the light. Blood was oozing from deep scratches on her hands. She felt no pain at all. The gun fired behind her, the shell whining away into the darkness. The silenced report echoed along the hillside. Despair gave her feet speed. She zigzagged through the trees and back onto the cart-track. It ran straight over the crest of the hill, down the other side and onto the downs.

Her bag was slowing her down. As soon as she had the chance she had to get rid of it. She slackened her pace, stumbling along the ruts. She couldn't keep this up much longer. But then nor could Benstead. Something rose in front of her and flashed into the darkness, running close to the ground. She went in the same direction as the motorcycle came to life again. Benstead passed her, riding very slowly and looking from side to side. The gun was tucked into the front of his windbreaker. Suddenly he accelerated, roared up the narrow track and vanished.

She lay where she had dropped for fully ten minutes, listening to the dwindling sound of the motor. And then it was gone, completely. She rose cautiously and started walking again. A quarter of an hour took her to the top of the hill.

She put her bag down and rested. A scab showed in the darkness below. After a while she moved down towards it. A five-acre patch had been cleared in the trees. A post-and-rail fence enclosed a corral and a cow byre. The track was thick with cow-pats. She spent another five minutes, standing in the trees, just staring at the building. She picked up a stone and advanced as far as the fence. She threw the stone awkwardly into the shadows beyond the open door. She crouched slightly, half expecting Benstead to emerge, stoop-shouldered and smiling. Nothing happened. She crawled through between the rails, sinking up to her ankles in churned mud reeking of ammonia. It was warm inside the building, the air sweet with the breath of twenty cows. Chains chinked softly as the nearest animals turned their heads to inspect her, jaws moving sideways as they continued to chew the cud. An owl hooted somewhere on the hillside. The sound reassured her — an indication that the forest was free of intruders.

A ladder in front of her led to a loft. She climbed up, spider webs dragging across her face. The loft was stacked with straw and hay. She sneezed violently, dust invading her nostrils. She sat down on the sagging floor and dragged her suitcase beside her. She emptied her handbag, transferring most of the things to her pockets. Passport, money, lipstick and mirror. She wrapped the four pieces of film in a tissue and put them inside her compact. Her handbag went inside her suitcase. She shoved this deep under the hay. Her hands were free now. She remembered the rain barrels standing outside the corral. She went down the ladder. A cow's hindquarters had swung across the way to the door. She went past it gingerly. She washed the dirt and blood from her face and hands, binding the deepest scratches with her handkerchief. Her mirror showed the skin stretched over high cheekbones, almost transparent. There was nothing that she could do with the rent in the knee of her slacks. She'd stop the first car she saw, with a tale of her own car somewhere in a ditch. She recrossed the corral and scraped the mud from her shoes.

The track dropped steeply. She could see the downs clearly — the giant chalk scars gouged in their sides. She hurried down, the steepness of the grade turning her walk into a shamble. The trees grew thinner on the unsheltered slopes. Branches shipped and creaked in the wind. She was near enough now to see the white furlong-markers along the gallops. She had almost reached the edge of the wood when Benstead stepped from behind an oak tree. She burst away in the opposite direction, screaming without knowing it. As she came out into the open, she had a vague impression of a car parked without lights. The headlamps came on; their brilliance took her full in the face as she ran towards them, shielding her eyes with her hand, still screaming for help.

Hamish Hunter

23 February 1967

DISC-BRAKES dragged the Rover to a halt. The jeep stopped behind it. A signpost showed in the headlamps, high in the hedge and pointing west. Both cars moved down the narrow cut-off to the village. Lights burned in the pub. A few cars stood in front. Men's voices were loud in the small saloon bar. Hunter waved Smith on, past the gate with a shingle, into the shadow of the manor-house wall. Here the lane widened, coming to an end in front of a NO ENTRY sign by the wrought-iron gates. He pointed back at the shingle.

"The cottage is down that path. You can't see it from here."

The driver of the jeep had parked with his lights tight against the rear of the Rover. He cut them, following Smith's lead. Smith leaned through his window, peering into the darkness behind the cottage.

"What lies up there?"

"Fields and a wood." Hunter watched as Smith climbed out, tight-mouthed. He went after him with the Director. Smith had a word with the driver of the jeep. O'Connor and another man slipped through the hedge, one each side of the cottage. A dog started barking as they worked their way through the neighboring gardens and round to the back. Hunter and Smith stopped at the gate. The cottage was in darkness.

Hunter spoke on impulse. "Why not let me go in first. I know every inch of the place."

Smith half-turned his head. It was too dark to see the expression on his face but his voice was curt.

"We'll go in together."

Hunter reached down, holding the tiny bell as he pushed the gate open. He felt in the mailbox. There were no letters, no key. The front door was unlocked. Smith turned the handle gingerly and threw the door wide. Both men flattened themselves against the wall, looking at one another across the open doorway. They waited there for a moment. Smith gestured with his small automatic. They stepped into the sitting room. A bottle of scotch was on the table, a full glass of whisky. Hunter ran down the passage. His own bedroom was empty — so was the bathroom. The kitchen door was locked and bolted. He unfastened the guest room on his way back. The curtains flapped in the open window. The bottom sash was raised as far as it would go. A hairbrush lay on the floor near the dresser, forgotten in its owner's haste to leave. He picked it up mechanically, showing it to Smith as he came back into the sitting room.

"Through the window," he said shortly. "She must have heard us."

They ran up the path, meeting O'Connor as he pushed his way through the hedge facing the pub. He said something to Smith in a low voice. The Director hurried over. Smith's face was grim.

"There are fresh tire-marks on the track going up into the woods."

He paused as a man came down the steps of the pub, looking from one to the other uncertainly. The man lifted a hand, recognizing Hunter.

"Well thank Christ *you're* there! What's all *this* in aid of, Hamish?"

Hunter pulled him aside. "Have you seen anyone in the cottage, Peter?"

Powell was doing his best to have a better look at Smith and the Director. They moved away a little.

"Seen anyone — of course I've seen someone. I went across to your place half an hour ago. I saw the lights from the pub. Your girl friend asked me in for a drink — acting very strangely indeed, I might add. I sat down. She excused herself. A couple of minutes later this weird character appeared from your bedroom. Before I knew what was happening, he had me out of the house saying that Wanda was drunk. He waited at the gate till he was sure I was back in the pub. I watched from behind the curtain. Out went the lights and I heard a motorcycle start up. Ran back to the cottage. Nobody!"

Hunter grabbed his arm. "A tall guy — elderly?"

Powell nodded. "Bald with a big nose. The first thing I noticed were his trousers. Bell-bottomed like a sailor's. In fact that's what I thought he was. I was trying to make up my mind whether or not I should call the police when I heard your voice. What's going on, Hamish?"

Hunter spoke rapidly. "I'll tell you later. There's no time now. Are the gates to the gallops unlocked?"

Powell thought a moment before answering. "Yes. You're

208

sure there's nothing you want me to do?" He looked beyond Hunter at the two men listening.

Hunter shook his head. "Go back home and turn on the television. You saw no one and you heard no one. If I need you I'll be up later."

Powell shrugged. He walked away towards the iron gates without looking back. Hunter pushed his hand through his hair. Smith and the General were watching him carefully.

"If you leave the jeep here, we can bottle them up in the woods. We'll reach the gallops before they will."

Smith loped across to the jeep. He gave some rapid instructions and came back wearing a walkie-talkie set slung round his neck.

"They're going to follow Benstead up the track. Let's get going."

The three men piled into the Rover. The powerful motor gunned its way along the sunken lane. Back on the main road, Hunter leaned over Smith's shoulder, directing him. A quarter-mile from the fork, the Canadian jumped out and held the gate open. The car rolled forward onto chalk-drained turf. Headlamps stared up the slope, picking out the white markers. They negotiated two more gates and came out on a level stretch of grass, a hundred yards wide. The turf here was scarred by horses' hooves. Off this and onto rougher ground, crawling up to the edge of the wood in low gear. Smith wheeled the Rover in a circle so that its front end was facing the end of the cart-track. He switched off his lights. The only sound was of the wind whining through the branches.

Smith turned round in his seat, breaking the silence. "I meant to tell you — your managing editor flies in from Toronto tomorrow. We'd like to do what we can to help."

Hunter shifted his feet. "Don't you think you've done enough, one way and another? You want to see Dunn, that's your business. I don't need you."

Smith's thin foxy face was patient. "Think about it, anyway. I made you a promise the other night in your flat. It still stands, however this affair turns out. Give me three days' grace and you'll have your story."

Hunter lifted a hand wearily. "Forget it, for God's sake. We're not making contact." He stopped, choked by the bitterness in his breast. The sound of someone running came on the wind. A woman's scream was shrill. Smith's fingers found the light switch. He threw it as Wanda burst out of the trees. She stumbled into the full glare of the headlamps, holding her hands in front of her eyes. Her voice was half scream, half shout. Two shots coughed in rapid succession. She jerked with each impact then pitched forward on her face, her arms stretched out towards the car.

Benstead stepped into the light, the silenced automatic still raised. He wavered as if gauging the distance from her body to the car. Then he swung round and lumbered back into the trees. The Deputy Director moved swiftly, reaching into the glove compartment. He shoved a service Webley into Hunter's hand.

"Keep the bloody thing pointed downwards till you use it."

They wrenched the doors open and ran to the prostrate body. Smith knelt by Wanda's side, lifting her chin. The first shell had drilled into her brain behind her right ear, mushrooming its way out in her forehead. Blood covered her entire face. The second shell had smashed into her shoulder blade. Smith wiped his hands on the grass.

"Dead before she hit the ground."

Hunter turned away, unable to look any more. He felt neither hatred nor pity — just empty. When he turned his head again, the two men were standing near the headlamps, looking at something in Smith's hand. Hunter recognized Wanda's compact.

He walked across to the dead woman and bent down, lifting her by the waist. He carried her out of the glare of the headlamps and laid her on the ground under the trees. He spread his handkerchief over her face, blotting out that part of his life. He came back into the light, the heavy pistol dangling in his hand. Smith showed him the contents of the compact. Hunter moved his head up and down, looking at the pieces of film blankly. Smith said something to the General and climbed into the car. Hunter leaned his back against the door, staring into the trees. Smith was speaking into the radiophone. Hunter heard the instructions without listening. Men were going to be pulled out of bed — photographers and dark-room experts — the whole weight of an organization thrown into the speedy development of four scraps of film. He moved aside, letting Smith climb into the car. Smith thumbed the safety catch of his snub-nosed automatic.

"I'm sending the film back to London as soon as I contact the jeep. Why don't you go with it. You look whacked."

The Canadian shook his head. Smith pressed the call button and used the walkie-talkie set. The answering voice was plain.

211

"Will do, sir. Yes. We heard the shots. There's no sign of him this side of the hill. We're about two hundred yards from the top, working up in extended order."

"He could be coming towards you," said Smith. "If you find the motorcycle, make sure you immobilize it. Over and out."

His eyes were concerned — almost friendly — as he looked at Hunter. "Let's get out of this — we've got to be mobile. And don't trade shots with him unless you have to. Leave that to us."

The General took the steering wheel. He took the big car slowly into the trees, driving up the cart-track behind blazing headlamps. Hunter and Smith stood behind on the overriders, flattened against the trunk. Smith used his microphone again, talking his men into a half-circle. The quiet unemotional voice, the narrowing noose, impressed Hunter. He imagined an animal lying in the undergrowth, heart and lungs bursting, listening to the sound of the beaters closing in. The thought was academic. He had no more or less pity for Benstead than for Wanda. A debt had to be settled. It was as simple as that.

He grabbed hard as the General braked. The cow byre was caught in the headlamps. The General leaned his head through the window.

"What do you think, Benjy?"

Smith hesitated, looking at Hunter. The Canadian jumped down. "I know the place. Turn your lights off and cover me."

He was climbing through the corral rails before they could stop him. The General extinguished the headlamps. Mud sucked at Hunter's shoes as he walked round to the back of the byre. The ground by the wall was firmer. He moved crabwise towards the open door. The cows stirred as they smelled him and heard him. White and dun shapes shifted in the twilight. He inched to the foot of the ladder, staring up at the dark square in the floor overhead. He went up, one rung at a time, the heavy gun pointed in front of him. The loft was empty. He squelched back through the mud. The two men were waiting at the rails. He climbed through, shaking his head.

"Nothing."

A shot shattered the surrounding silence — the coughed report of a weapon that is silenced. They ran across the clearing and took cover behind the car. Seconds later the jeep appeared, O'Connor at the wheel. The windshield was starred, a hole drilled through it near his head. He braked hard, sprang out and came over at the double. Splinters of glass silvered his track suit. He spoke breathlessly.

"He's up there, somewhere on the left, sir. He'll have to come down this way. We've got him bottled up on the other side."

Smith pushed the compact holding the film into O'Connor's hand.

"They're waiting for this at number seventeen. Get it there as quickly as you can. You stop for nothing, sergeant. Is that understood, *nothing!*"

O'Connor saluted, wheeled and raced back to the jeep. It careered down the track towards the downs and the London road.

Hunter bent down, scraping the mud from his shoes. When

213

he straightened up, the General was studying him curiously. The older man opened the door.

"Let's flush this bugger out of his hole." He took the wheel. Smith and Hunter stood behind again on the overriders. They were halfway across the clearing when a motorcycle engine roared above. The General wrenched at the wheel, trying to turn the heavy car. He stalled the motor in his haste. Benstead appeared over the crest of the hill. He came down at them fast, bending low over the handlebars. The gun jumped in Smith's hand. The shells smacked wide of their target. The General had the Rover moving again. The rear wheels found traction. The car shot forward at speed, trapping Benstead in the powerful headlamps. He swerved blindly. The motorcycle left the track, Benstead still sitting like a circus performer. Both wheels flew off the ground. They heard the impact of metal against wood fifteen yards away. Flame followed the explosion, lighting the forest in every direction. They ran forward and dragged Benstead clear of the blazing gasoline. His head lolled at a strange angle. He tried to say something as they lifted him. They laid him on the ground by the side of the car. Blood was starting to come from his nose. The General looked down at him, his face expressionless. O'Connor's men were thrashing through the trees towards the flames. Smith ran to meet them.

There was fresh blood on Hunter's sleeve. He stared at it, glad of the wind on his face. He walked over to the car, leaned in and put his gun on the seat next to the General. He started to walk up the track. Footsteps came after him. Smith caught him by the arm, turning him.

"Where do you think you're going?"

Hunter removed the hand from his sleeve. The gesture was weary but definite.

"Home. And don't bother following me there. You and I don't have anything to say to one another any more."

He walked on, his eyes on the patch of sky ahead. It would be better on the other side of the hill. It always was.

›› If you've enjoyed this book and would like to discover more great vintage crime and thriller titles, as well as the most exciting crime and thriller authors writing today, visit: ››

The Murder Room
Where Criminal Minds Meet

themurderroom.com